THE TRICK SHOT

Also by the Author

The Last Lawmen
The Indian Fighter's Return
The Deserter Troop
Escape from Yuma
The Surrogate Gun
The Rough Rider
Once a Legend
Rebels West!
Tiger Butte
Lynch's Revenge
Sergeant Gringo
Dead Man's Medal

THE TRICK SHOT

Jack Cummings

Walker and Company
New York

All the characters and events portrayed in this work are fictitious.

First published in the United States of America in 1996 by Walker Publishing Company, Inc.

Published simultaneously in Canada by Thomas Allen & Son Canada, Limited, Markham, Ontario

Library of Congress Cataloging-in-Publication Data

Cummings, Jack, 1925–
The trick shot / Jack Cummings.
p. cm.
ISBN 0-8027-4153-3
I. Title.
PS3553.U444T45   1996
813'.54—dc20   95-46723
                        CIP

Printed in the United States of America

2   4   6   8   10   9   7   5   3   1

THE TRICK SHOT

PROLOGUE

Goldfield, Nevada, June 1907

IN THE FOUR years since its discovery, the renowned gold strike location had grown into a mining town of 15,000 people. It now had a rail line through Tonopah from Carson City, and telegraph, banks, stores, hotels, saloons, and a newly built Hippodrome Variety Theatre.

John Drake never knew why it happened. There he was, one of the best six-gun trick-shot artists in show business, standing twenty-five feet away from Molly, his bride-to-be. Her handsome left profile was turned toward him, her carmined lips holding the lighted cigarette that was his target.

And he missed.

The bullet severed her carotid artery and she died moments later in his arms. That was the day he hung up his guns.

Theirs had been the featured final act of a daily program that offered over a dozen performers that included acrobats, a ventriloquist, a juggler, a wire walker, a magician, a song-and-dance man, and others.

All of whom attended the funeral three days later.

And all of whom tried hard, but hopelessly, to offer condolences that, in his agony of remorse, drew no response from Drake. It was as if he had died himself.

In the days that followed, when they looked for him they could not find him. He had disappeared, on horseback, with only a few provisions.

Disappeared somewhere into the Nevada desert.

CHAPTER 1

HE RODE MOSTLY in a blank-minded state of shock.

Those were the periods of relief.

Other times there intruded a mental review of the component parts of his performance, a performance that should have ended with the extinguishing of a lighted cigarette. Not of Molly's life.

He had many stunts worked out for his trick-shot routine, all done against a backstop on stage. First came his shooting at targets held in wooden holders, where he split playing cards turned edgewise toward him, snuffed out candles, and drew a sketch of an Indian head on a sizable blank sheet of cardboard with bullet holes, along with a variety of other tricks.

Some tricks were repeated with his back turned. Sighting into a mirror, his arms folded across his chest, he'd have a gun in one hand and a mirror in the other.

Then Molly, who had been setting the targets for him, entered actively into the act. She stood in front of the backstop with the contours of her lovely body closely outlined with twelve inflated small balloons, which he destroyed in rapid single-action fire, using two guns, one in each hand.

All through his performance he kept up a steady patter while he reloaded, becoming silent only when he shot.

And eventually he came to the final trick where she stood with the cigarette in her mouth.

Now, as his mind came to that last finale, he felt he never wanted to talk again.

*　　*　　*

He rode three days, and the water in the canteens he had shared with the horse was gone. He knew another day might see him dead, and the horse too.

That bothered him. The horse dying, not himself.

At first he had followed a little-used stagecoach trace that went southeasterly. Somewhere along that way, he had heard, was a deserted small mining location. Some old prospector he had met in Goldfield had mentioned its existence. A ghost town now, the oldster had said. A fact that now offered a lure of the oblivion that Drake craved.

He had forgotten the ghost town's name. It was of no matter. What mattered was that he find solitude, away from the eyes of others.

Eventually he lost the trace in a confusing region of dry desert washes and, unable to regain it, went blindly on.

In the wasteland heat, his thirst became a constant.

He recalled the old desert rat had spoken of a spring at the location. Which meant nothing now, if he could not find it.

If the horse was dying of thirst, he could lessen its misery.

He could shoot it.

The thought shocked him. Kill again with a gun?

The horse staggered, and Drake slipped from the saddle and halted in the scant shade of a Joshua tree. He peered ahead, hoping to see some sign of weathered structures. But the desert here was heavy with creosote bush, rather than sage, and his vision was limited.

When he went on, he led the horse, tugging at the reins when it periodically lagged.

They went on and on that way, fatigue and thirst driving all thought from him.

Then, gradually, he became aware that the reins he held were slack, and the horse was beside him and crowding past. It could mean only one thing—water close ahead.

And now he could see the cluster of sun-darkened wooden shacks.

It had been one of those many short-lived Nevada strikes with early promise and limited return.

Across from the shacks a little distance rose a hill with an adit into a mine shaft. Others were visible above and below on either side. None of the tailings slopes were extensive.

At the east end of a street was an adjoining rise of knolls, between two of which nestled a scrawl of cottonwood trees, indicating a possible spring.

But the horse had passed him by, fighting the bit as it tried to break free, and that was a surer sign.

Drake's first few days in the ghost town were passed in a blank existence. When he saw a paint-peeled fallen sign in front of one of the shacks, *Tawich Mercantile,* he recalled that Tawich was the name of the deserted town.

A brief glance within revealed that it had been emptied of goods. Since his supplies had dwindled to a few cans of food, he took his carbine and lay in wait near the spring for game to show.

He waited a long time, and nothing came.

Then a lone antelope doe appeared.

Deerlike tan, white chest and rump, black hoofs. She was a yard high at the shoulders, but Drake noticed she seemed almost dainty in her movements. He aimed the carbine at her—but he did not press the trigger.

She appeared unaware of his presence as she drank from the spring.

He held his gun sight on her. Then he lowered the weapon, seizing upon the rationale that he still had food for a few meals. Yet he knew that was not the real reason for his reluctance to shoot. He knew it had to do with what had happened to Molly. What he didn't know was what to do about it.

*   *   *

The following day a stagecoach approached. Drake saw the dust rising above it and was alert and watchful. He stood at the edge of the town, waiting as it pulled in.

The driver, alone on the box without a swamper, looked down. "What the hell you doing here, friend?"

"Existing," Drake said. "You on a regular run?"

"Every couple of weeks," the driver said. "Round trip out of Goldfield to a place called Antelope Wells, thirty-five miles down the road." He paused. "Say, ain't I seen you somewheres before?"

"You carrying any foodstuff you can spare?"

"Not hardly. Just them two passengers you see staring out of the coach at you."

Drake flicked his glance to a couple of business-suited men at the window openings. "Who supplies the town at Antelope Wells?"

"Freighters use a road up from the south at Beatty. You out of grub?"

"Almost."

"Got any money?"

"Some."

"Say! I know who you are now. Seen your picture posted in front of the Hippodrome. The pistol shooter, ain't you?"

Drake gave him a reluctant short nod, glanced again at the men in the cab, saw a quick interest touch their faces.

"Listen," the driver said, "I'll be coming back this way in a couple days. You give me a food list and enough to cover it, plus make it worth my while, and I'll bring grub to you." He paused, then added, "You show folks get good pay, I understand."

Drake fished a piece of paper and a pencil out of his pocket and scribbled out a list.

The driver had set his brake and climbed down, and the two passengers got out of the coach and walked a few paces away to urinate. Finished, they eyed Drake with scarcely veiled curiosity. Neither of them spoke.

Drake handed the jehu his list and drew a large-denomination bill from a wallet.

"You figure this will cover it?"

"I reckon. My name's Joe Joad, Mr. Drake." He reached for the money, tucked it and the list into his shirt pocket, then said, "You familiar with this country?"

"No."

"Well, if you get in trouble, there's a swing station seven, eight miles down the road, where we change the team. Can't see it for them low hills." He paused. "Got one every fourteen miles or so." He paused again. "Hell, you must've passed two of them on your way out here."

Drake said, "I started on a trace out of Goldfield, but I lost it in some wash-cut country. Never found it again until I was lucky enough to blunder into it here."

Joad said, "Man, you must have been out of your mind, riding into this desert the way you done." He gave Drake a hard stare, but when Drake said nothing, his look softened some, and he said, "Maybe I understand how that could be, Mr. Drake. I read what happened to you in the newspaper."

He turned and climbed up on the coach as the two passengers entered below. As he drove off, one of the men twisted his head out of a coach window to look back at Drake. Then they were gone.

Drake stood looking after them, wondering if the knowledge of where he was would be spread by Joad or the passengers.

He hoped not. He needed to be alone. Far from any reminders of what had happened. His guilt and remorse were too agonizing.

Even worse was the doubt, uncertainty about what had gone wrong. Had his skill suddenly failed him—or was the accident caused by a "hang fire" in his revolver? Was there a deficient charge in the fatal bullet?

Regardless of what the explanation was, one thing was undeniable. He was the one who had fired the fatal shot.

On the third day after Joad left, Drake was completely out of food. The stage driver had said he would be back in a couple of days. Was he held up or had he been lying? Could he have bypassed the ghost town by an alternative trail on the return trip?

The thought drove Drake to take his carbine again to the waterhole and wait, screened in the brush, for thirsty game.

The game came. Startlingly, it was the same lone antelope.

Once again he sighted the weapon for a kill.

And once again he could not force himself to shoot. The animal drank its fill and trotted off.

Drake went back to the quarters he had taken in one of the shacks and lay there on his blanket, pondering his inability to kill game. Perhaps he was not yet hungry enough . . .

Joad came the next day.

This time he had no passengers. He said, "I was held over, expecting a couple, but they canceled out. I got a load of grub for you, though."

He helped Drake unload it, then said, "I didn't tell anybody who this was for. I figured you'd want it that way."

"What about the two that were with you?" Drake said.

"Can't say. Didn't see them after I let them off in front of the hotel." He paused. "Town there may grow, may not. There's been a ledge or two of high-grade ore assayed, and the place is full of would-be leasers, like that pair you seen, who are there to check out the prospects, I reckon. Men like that are all business, I doubt they gave a second thought to your situation."

Joad studied Drake's face. It showed him nothing.

"I'll be on my way," he said. "See you in a couple of weeks."

"I appreciate it."

"Yeah, sure," the driver said, wondering if the man intended to stay there forever.

CHAPTER 2

Nevada State Prison, Carson City, July

DURING THE NIGHTLY lockup procedure, fifteen convicts overpowered the guards. They broke into the guards' arsenal and took weapons for themselves.

In the action that followed, they liberated a dozen more inmates, killed five officials, and fled down the California-Nevada border. Most of them were soon caught and sent back to their cells. Some were killed by the pursuing guards.

But three escaped.

Their survival was not a bit of random luck. One lifer, Jack Shaw, sensing a breakout was imminent, had made a separate plan for himself and two cohorts.

He had long ruminated on where he would flee if he got out.

"Not California," he'd told Tom Huff and Mike Longo, both lifers too.

"Why not?" Longo had asked.

"Because that's where anybody wants to get out of Nevada thinks to go."

So when the break came, he slipped away with them to the outskirts of town to remain hidden until full dark fell. They stayed under cover until they could make their way to the loading yards of the Carson and Colorado Railroad that linked up now at the former southern terminus at Sodaville with the new extension of the Tonopah and Goldfield line. Shaw had had the foresight to learn the timetable, so they would be sure not to be too late for the nightly departure of the train.

He had picked his partners with this in mind, among other things. Both, like himself had done some "riding the rods" under railcars. Railroad fares were high in Nevada—stowing away under the cars had been a trick of the trade for itinerant mine workers on their way to a job destination. Although none of these three were miners, they too had used the method on occasion.

Now Shaw led them hurriedly through the back streets and reached the string of freight and passenger cars a scant fifteen minutes before its departure time.

Each man waited in the bordering darkness, then slipped, as chance came, to crawl under separate cars and sprawl his body on the brake rods.

Ensconced underneath they felt the train start up and slowly reach its cruising speed beyond the town limits.

At that moment Shaw felt deservedly smug. No guards had followed them. Everyone had been too caught up in chasing after the body of escapees on the run for California.

Not Jack Shaw, by god. His destination was Arizona, and he planned to reach there by crossing the vast Ralston Desert on horseback.

The three convicts rode their way down the line to the railroad division point at Mina, where they debarked the agonizing brake rods while some cargo was transferred to the Southern Pacific narrow gauge line that veered westerly toward California.

In the confusion of a town rife with wagon freighting to and from vicinity mine destinations, Shaw and his men robbed a professional gambler as he left a saloon and took a shortcut through an alley.

It was luck their victim was carrying five hundred dollars in currency.

The victim had some luck too—he regained consciousness after the blow to the head from a heavy rock. But he couldn't describe whoever had hit him because he had never seen his assailant.

With some of the money, Shaw bought three passenger fares to Tonopah, seventy miles to the southeast.

The ticket clerk eyed his convict garb somewhat dubiously but seemed to convince himself it was just some more of the varied clothing worn by freighters and tradesmen. He handed over the tickets without comment. Shaw was a big man, not one to argue with.

Shaw had caught his look, though, and was glad that state prisoners now wore plain prison gray, unlike the black and white stripes of earlier years.

Tonopah, in the seven years since the rich deposits of its silver lode were discovered, had become a regular city.

It now had fancy hotels, electric and water companies, five banks, several schools, scores of other buildings, and two daily newspapers.

Shaw changed his plan and they slipped off the train in Tonopah instead of Goldfield. They inquired the location of the nearest livery.

There Shaw bought mounts and saddles for them.

The ostler eyed them curiously as they made their selections. Three unshaved customers who appeared to have no belongings besides the rough clothing they wore were enough to raise some suspicion.

His manner eased when Shaw brought out his roll of currency and paid his price after only brief haggling.

"You boys got some good riding stock," he said then.

"We just got into town," Shaw said. "Want to ride around the diggings and look them over."

"Sure," the liveryman said. With their money in his pocket he didn't ask why they had not simply rented.

Shaw left quickly with the others, leading them to another part of town before stopping at a mercantile.

They entered and ordered what supplies Shaw thought they needed, including three sacks of foodstuff and two canteens each.

The storekeeper said, "You boys figuring on crossing the desert?"

When none of them answered, he did not press the question.

But once outside, Huff took up the subject.

"Going to be a damn far piece across the desert before we reach Arizona," he said.

"We could've took the train down another twenty-five miles to Goldfield," Longo said.

"That rail clerk back in Mina got me worrying," Shaw said. "I kept thinking we best not push our luck too long. If he got a telegraph about the escape after we left, he might have sent out an alarm."

The first day out of Tonopah, they made only fifteen miles; after a cold meal, they threw themselves onto their blankets, saddle sore and exhausted.

After varying periods of confinement, this was a physical ordeal for all of them. There had been hard labor at times at the prison, but it had been a long time since they'd ridden horseback.

They rose the next morning stiff and truculent, a mood not dispelled even by bacon and coffee.

Once saddled up, they rode in silence.

It was Longo who finally broke it. "Dammit, Shaw! I'm beginning to think this is worse than what we been used to."

Shaw scowled. Longo was a good man to have on your side in a showdown, but his tendency to gripe got on his nerves at times.

"It'll get better," Shaw said, "soon as your butt gets calloused."

Longo made no reply to that.

They rode on, silent again.

The desert sage was thinner here, but the creosote bush grew thicker. That's the way Nevada was, he thought. Sage country in the north, creosote bush in the south. And scattered Joshua trees.

He had outlawed a lot of years in different parts of the state. He was nearing forty now, older by five years maybe than Huff, and about ten years older than Longo.

He was hurting, too. But he'd get trail-toughened soon enough. When he did, he'd be tougher than either of his companions—though they'd be tough enough. That's why he'd picked them for what he had in mind once they reached Arizona.

Even now, despite his fatigue, he was wishing they'd had time and freedom from risk to remain in Tonopah long enough to visit crib row.

For a spell he eased his discomfort by thinking of women. Jeez! he had been a long time without one. All three of them had.

One crib visit wouldn't have been enough for any of them, though. They could have spent a week there. And then some.

CHAPTER 3

A PAIUTE GIRL named Henie was riding a borrowed horse eastward from Goldfield into the desert. She was alone and on her way to visit her brother, a long day's ride away. He was working a gold claim on which he had filed in the foothills of the Cactus Range.

She had been working in Goldfield as a hotel maid but had been laid off when the hotel ownership changed hands.

She was looking forward to seeing Tagee—they had always been close, with an independence of spirit that had driven them to leave the Walker River Reservation to seek a life of their own as they reached maturity. Both had found jobs working as menials for various whites and came to speak English well. Henie, though, spoke it far better than her brother.

Initially they stayed together, Tagee, who was two years older, acting more or less as her guardian, until he went to work as a mucker in a mine. Then he decided to try his luck at prospecting.

As he worked his claim now, they were separated for weeks at a time, meeting only when he went into the boomtown for supplies.

Just once he had taken her to see his diggings, from which with backbreaking toil he had been able to extract just enough gold float to keep going.

So she knew the way and had promised she would visit the claim on the day following her scheduled job termination.

She had got the loan of the horse from a livery owner

who had partly grubstaked Tagee, hoping the enterprising young Paiute might develop something profitable.

It was a time when almost everybody had gold fever— businessmen as well as prospectors.

Tagee's claim was on the westerly slope of the mountain foothills, with a spring nearby from which he hauled water and where there was forage for horse or burro.

The gold was scant thus far, and the work hard, but he kept at it. Tagee, busy digging as always, got some solace in the thought that Henie was due today for her visit. It was something to lighten the drudgery of his work.

Except she never arrived.

At first he was just disappointed, thinking there might be a reason she was delayed.

Perhaps the hotel owner had granted her a few more days of employment. But he felt that was unlikely. Maybe she was sick. That was unlikely, too. She was a tall, slim girl, but robust, and she shook off most minor illnesses easily, if she caught them at all.

He worried through one more day. In the late afternoon he saddled up his own horse and took the faint trail back toward Goldfield.

Halfway there he came upon the hoofprints of the mount she had previously borrowed and ridden.

There was a distinguishing mark to them that he had noted then and later discussed with the grubstaking livery owner: a chronic dropped sole due to inflammation of the coffin bone within the left forehoof. When it was not in remission it caused a mild lameness apparent in the hoofprint.

The owner had shrugged it off—the sometime handicap limited the horse's rental value, which was why he loaned it free to Henie on occasion.

Having mentioned his passing concern, Tagee dropped the subject. It would not do to offend his benefactor.

Now, as he sat studying the scene, his eyes swept the

other prints, those he could assume were left by three male riders.

Three men who had intersected her path, coming down from the north.

And there were signs of struggle.

He sat staring in horror, gathering their significance.

She had been dragged from her saddle. She had been thrown to the ground by a dismounted, booted man. She had fought him wildly until his sheer weight subdued her.

Tagee's eyes searched for sign of blood, but the desert dust had obliterated whatever there might have been.

But there was a remnant of torn undergarments.

She would have fought until knocked unconscious, he thought. According to the tracks they rode off southeast, taking her, probably lashed to the saddle of her own horse.

Taking her along for further use.

Inside Tagee, rage grew.

CHAPTER 4

JOHN DRAKE'S AGONY did not lessen.

Each day passed as did the one before. Time did not heal.

There was no break in the endless weeks.

Until the day the three riders rode in, leading a Paiute girl tied to her saddle. It was just past noon.

The big man, leader of the three, greeted him with false joviality.

"Hey, friend, you all alone here?"

His eyes were sweeping the shacks even as he asked.

Drake did not answer, noting the way the girl was bound.

The big man pretended not to be offended by Drake's silence and said, "If so, I'd guess you'd welcome company."

When Drake still did not speak, his manner changed quickly.

"One of them half-crazy prospectors, are you?" He paused. "Say, maybe you got a claim full of high-grade gold here someplace."

"No gold here," Drake said. "Town went *borrasca* years ago."

Longo said, "Hey, Shaw, ask him about groceries. I'm hungry."

"How about it?" Shaw said. "You got food?"

Drake said, "You got a sack hanging on each of your saddles. My guess is you've got your own."

Shaw's voice hardened. "I didn't ask what your guess was. Besides, we've picked up a unexpected guest along the way. You wouldn't want to see her go hungry, would you?"

"I can spare you a meal," Drake said.

17

"Now we'd sure as hell appreciate that, friend," Shaw said. "Trot it out."

"You going to untie the girl there?"

"Why?"

"To eat, of course."

"Sure," Shaw said. "We want to keep her alive and well." He turned away then and spoke to one of the others. "Huff, untie the Injun."

Huff moved to do so, then dragged her roughly from the saddle, so that she fell flat on the ground.

Drake said, "No way to treat a lady."

"Ain't a lady," Shaw said. "She's an Injun."

"Makes no difference," Drake said.

"Friend, you looking for trouble?"

Longo spoke up, "Shaw, don't get too rough with him till we know where his grub is stored."

The girl scrambled to her feet as if she feared Huff might rape her where she lay.

Drake saw that and frowned.

Shaw noted his expression and said, "Don't get yourself involved in something, friend. You just bring out some eatables. We'll lay over a spell, being a bit tired of riding. And I see you got a waterhole, end of the street there, and maybe some forage better than sage for our horses." He paused. "We'll be on our way tomorrow. I ain't in a mind to linger."

Then, as Drake started away to get food, Shaw held up a hand to halt him. "Just one thing more, friend. Don't try to give us any trouble. You can see we got guns, and we know how to use them. I've a mind to leave you in peace, if you cooperate."

"What about the girl?" Drake said.

"What about her?"

"Looks like she's been rough-treated."

Shaw scowled. "You got more guts than brains to bring that up. Don't involve yourself in what we're doing—that's what I meant by cooperate."

Drake started away without comment.

Longo said to Shaw, "Maybe we ought to shoot the son-ofabitch."

"No," Shaw said. "I got him pegged as just another desert prospector. A lot of them get a little addled in the head from the life they lead. I figure he's harmless."

"I don't," Longo said.

"Let me tell you how it is with me," Shaw said. "I'm giving him a chance to behave." He hesitated, then said, "A few years back I was caught without water in one of these deserts. Dying. One like him come upon me and saved me, and I ain't ever forgot it."

"He don't look much like a prospector to me."

"Why else would he be living out here?" Shaw said. "Anyhow he reminds me of that other one. So we leave him alone."

"All right," Longo said, "you're the boss." But he sounded puzzled, as if he found it hard to believe Shaw could have this feeling.

Shaw noted this and said, "If he acts up, I could change my mind in a hurry."

Huff pushed the Paiute girl over toward him.

"So be it," Longo said.

Back in his quarters, gathering food to feed them, Drake had a chance to hide his money belt. But first he took out a few dollars and shoved them in his pocket.

These were hardcases, he was sure. Who else would be treating a woman the way they were?

It bothered him mightily. For the first time since the tragedy in Goldfield, he was concerned about something other than what happened at the Hippodrome.

Perhaps because it was a woman victimized, he thought. Suppose it were Molly at their mercy?

That thought brought it all back again, overshadowing the concern he felt for the Paiute girl. But only briefly.

Now, as they hunkered about making their meal from

the cans he had brought them, he noted she had found a spot several yards away. Her face showed both fear and hate, he saw. And something else—a swelling over her left cheekbone.

From somebody's fist, he thought.

He had not noticed the bruise before, and he wondered if she'd had it when they'd arrived. Or had it been dealt her while he was in his quarters?

He wanted to talk to her, but moving in her direction, he was stopped by Shaw. "Hey, you! Stay away from the Injun!"

Drake saw her eyes meet his and hold them. Saw a beseeching there, then hopelessness.

He turned back to face the big intruder.

Shaw scowled. "I told you not to get involved with her."

"Why is she with you?" Drake said.

Shaw hesitated, then said, "She was lost on the desert, friend. Riding all alone back there, when lucky for her, we come upon her. Couldn't just leave her that way, so we brung her with us."

"Tied to her saddle?"

"She was a little addled by the sun, I guess. Had the idea we was outlaws or something and tried to break away. We had to restrain her for her own good." Shaw paused. "You can see she don't trust us even yet. Sitting over there apart like she is."

Drake looked at the girl again. What Shaw said could be true, he thought. She was obviously distraught. Perhaps her facial bruises had been somehow acquired by her own actions.

Longo said, "Shaw, why don't we lay over a day. Break into riding again easy-like."

Shaw appeared to give it some thought. "Might be we will."

Drake was silent. He wanted them gone, though the girl's situation still bothered him. Something didn't seem right.

Shaw looked at him and said, "Friend, you don't talk much. Most prospectors I met in the past been gabby as hell. Comes from being alone so much. Talk to their damn burros, I understand. And that's another thing—don't seem you even have one."

Again, Drake made no comment.

A thought seemed to strike Shaw then, and he said, "Say, you hiding out from the law?"

"No," Drake said.

"By god, you're a weird one. But you put me in mind of one I once knew." He paused. "You finding any prospects around here?"

"Not yet," Drake said. He realized now he might ward off Shaw's curiosity by playing the role of what the man assumed he was. "I still got hopes."

Shaw guffawed. "Your kind always do. Just like the one I mentioned."

"I guess so."

As they finished eating, Longo said again, "We going to lay over a day, like I asked?"

Shaw pondered a moment, then said to Drake, "You been in Goldfield lately?"

"It's been several weeks."

"What kind of law they got there?"

"Law? Same law they got everywhere in Nevada."

"I mean law*men*," Shaw said.

"Constable named Claude Inman and several deputies handle things in and around the town area. He's got a reputation for doing the job well."

"Constable, huh? Local lawdog. That's all?"

The questioning bolstered Drake's suspicion the intruders were on the dodge. If so, he wanted to be rid of them before they got ideas of making a victim of him.

He said, "No. The Esmeralda county sheriff has his headquarters in town, too. Ingalls is his name."

"Ingalls?"

"You know of him?"

Shaw was silent for a moment, then nodded and said, "I knew of him a few years back. He was in Hawthorne then."

"I think so," Drake said. "He's been the sheriff for a long time, the way I heard it."

"Yeah," Shaw said. "I heard that too."

Longo said, "Hell, I read something about him in a Carson newspaper a while back. He's an old man now. Too old to go chasing around horseback. Ought to retire."

Shaw gave him a quick, disapproving frown.

Longo caught the look and went silent.

Drake said, "He's got several deputies of his own. Tough men. Handle problems around the mines."

Shaw said, "Town's grown big lately, I reckon."

"Fifteen thousand people, they say," Drake said. "They've even got an exchange for trading mine stocks."

"Stock exchange?" Shaw said. "Got telegraph, too, then? Get all kinds of news from outside, I guess."

"That they do," Drake said.

"Very interesting to hear," Shaw said. He paused, looked at Longo, and said, "Well, we'll be leaving come first light tomorrow, I reckon."

Longo made no objection.

Drake went back to his quarters.

He was certain now that they were outlaws.

And that the Indian girl was being held against her will.

But was Shaw's story of how they had found her true— lost and disoriented? If so, why did Shaw prevent him from talking to her?

Drake did not want to face up to what seemed to be the truth: Shaw was lying. Lying to cover the real reason they kept the girl with them.

What could he do about it?

He went across the room and withdrew from a sack the belt and pistol he wore in the act he had performed so many times in his show career. It was a small-caliber revolver on a frame resembling a Colt Peacemaker. Specially made for him.

Thirty-two caliber. Shaw was a big man. And he had two partners. To kill with it, you had to put the bullet into a vulnerable place.

Like the bullet that wrongly struck Molly.

He dropped the gun as if it had burned his hand.

He eyed his carbine leaning in a corner but did not go to it. He had a .45 Colt too, but he did not go for it either.

Instead he lay on his blanket and stared at the rough roof boards above him.

He began to reflect on what he had told the outlaw leader about the lawmen in Goldfield. Actually he did not know too much. He had only been there a couple of weeks before the tragedy occurred.

To his knowledge though, neither the constable nor the elderly sheriff ever concerned himself with crimes outside the boomtown area. Goldfield itself had enough robberies, thefts, and burglaries by a criminal element of nonmining gold seekers to keep the lawmen busy locally.

He had not told this to the outlaw, of course, wanting him to worry about possible pursuit.

That part seemed to be working.

As to what else he should do, he had no answer. An hour went by, then another. And suddenly a figure rushed through the open doorway, ran by where he lay, and huddled in a corner beyond. He leaped to his feet.

The Paiute girl said, "Help me. Please help me."

He stared at her.

"Can you help me?" she said.

"What's wrong?" he said.

"They are doing bad things to me again," she said.

"Bad things? Who, Shaw?"

"All three!"

"The bastards!" he said.

"You help?"

"What can I do?" he said, and felt shame as he said it.

A big shadow filled the doorway, then halted.

Drake stared, and saw it was Shaw. Shaw moving into the room, moving toward the girl.

Without thought, Drake stepped into his path and felt Shaw's right fist smash like a sledgehammer against his jaw. He went down, felt a boot heel stomp on his head as Shaw went by, and heard a slap land, with the cracking sound of a freighter's whip, on the girl's face.

He heard her cry of pain, then the thud of a fist followed by a sob.

He struggled to his feet and launched himself against the crouched back as Shaw bent low to reach the fallen girl with a series of fore- and backhanded slaps.

The big man whirled as he straightened, throwing Drake off and against a wall hard enough to stun him.

Shaw pulled his gun from its holster, moved close, and began pistol-whipping Drake's head and shoulders.

The last thing Drake felt was the smashing gun barrel as it beat him into a pit of darkness.

As it happened, he seemed to hear Shaw saying, "I told you not to get involved. Why didn't you listen?"

He awoke in the night to a throbbing headache and knife-like jabs of pain in his shoulders. He did not try to move, and presently he lost consciousness again.

This happened again, and still again.

It was full daylight when he awoke the last time. He lay still in undiminished pain, trying to recall what had happened.

Slowly the recollection came.

He twisted his head, trying to look about him, half-expecting to see Shaw waiting there to continue beating him.

A vagrant thought came to him. Why had the big outlaw only beat him? He'd had a gun in hand but had used it only as a club instead of triggering it.

Not unlike me, he thought. Something had held Shaw back.

He stopped thinking then and struggled to roll over. He rose to his knees and got to his feet. He lost his balance and would have fallen had he not struck the adjacent wall. He stood there, leaning against it, dizzy and breathing hard.

The girl, he thought. Where is she?

The outlaws would have taken her again, of course. To use.

He remembered now how Shaw had been slapping her around.

Why? Because she had come to Drake, asking for his help.

A slow anger began building in him, turning to rage. An anger at witnessing a woman victimized. Maybe it grew because of Molly too.

He wanted to do something about it.

Almost without further thought, he began to get ready. He was slow about it, because of his physical hurts. But he kept on because it was hours since first light, when Shaw had scheduled the outlaws' leaving.

Then he want to saddle his horse.

It was gone from the weathered stable where he had taken it after letting it graze near the spring area before the intruders arrival.

They had taken it, he was sure.

Half-delirious with pain, he would not be stopped. Taking filled canteens, his holstered show pistol, the larger-calibered gun stuck in his belt, and carrying his carbine, he started walking south on the stage trace.

Joad had said there was a coach swing station a short distance down that way. And hoof prints of the outlaws were plain before him.

Keeping a grasp on those two facts, he trudged on, no further plans in his mind.

A long time later he came out of a narrow pass through

low hills and saw the sun-blasted wood shack of the station, a nearby stable, and a granary. A team of horses were in a crude corral.

A pair of men he assumed were the stockkeepers exited the station and stood watching his approach.

When he got within speaking distance, the taller of the two said, "You lose your horse?"

"Stolen," Drake said, lowering his carbine butt to the ground.

"Yeah," the station man said. "You the man Joad told us was living at the ghost town?"

Drake nodded.

The shorter tender said, "Come on into the station out of the sun." He paused. "You look plumb beat."

The other one was studying Drake's swollen, lacerated face, and he said, "Beat by more than the heat, by the looks of you."

Drake said nothing as he followed them in.

There were a few crudely built chairs sitting about the room, and Drake sank gratefully into one.

He said then, "Any riders come through ahead of me?"

"They came through," one of them said. "But they didn't stop. Leading a saddled horse, might have been yours."

Again Drake nodded.

"Three hard-looking hombres. And leading something else—a Injun gal tied to her saddle."

"That's them," Drake said.

The station keeper was studying his face again and said, "You ain't foolish enough to be chasing them?"

When Drake did not answer, he said, "That Injun gal mean something to you?"

Drake surprised himself with his reply. "Yes."

"Well, sir, I see you come well armed for what might happen if you catch them." His eyes studied Drake's weapons and the belt strapped around his waist.

"That's a fancy gun rig you're wearing. Looks like something out of a Wild West show." Drake ignored the comment and said, "Have you got a horse I can buy?"

"No riding stock. Nearest place you could get one is Antelope Wells."

"How far?"

"Twenty-eight, thirty miles. A long walk in the sun, with that load of guns and such you're carrying. If you wait a few days, Joad will be coming back this way from Goldfield. But I reckon you're in a hurry."

"I am."

"I figured."

"I'll push on."

"Fill your canteens before you leave. And good luck."

Night fell with a lessening of the heat, and he kept on, but with legs cramping now from the unaccustomed effort. Finally, his knotted muscles threw him headlong into the sand.

He lay there unmoving for a long time and eventually fell into exhausted sleep.

The sun awoke him. He got up and resumed his walk. Somewhere ahead was another swing station. The hours passed, and he kept looking ahead for sight of it, but the undulations of the terrain obstructed his view.

He had stopped for a brief rest, when for no reason he glanced back and saw a horseman approaching.

The rider came close enough to make eye contact with Drake before he halted.

He sat there in silence, no expression on his face.

An Indian face, Drake thought.

Faintly familiar?

The Indian finally spoke. "You got many guns. I want only pass on my way."

Drake saw he had a carbine in a saddle scabbard. "I have no objection," he said.

The Indian nodded and started to ride by, then halted. "I seen picture of you. In Goldfield. In the newspaper. You man who killed his woman."

The flat statement chilled Drake despite the baking sun. "An accident," he said.

"Sure. Everybody know that. But what you doing in desert? You got no horse. I read tracks. You walk from ghost town. Why?"

"You must have read the other tracks, too."

"I read from way back. Back where three bad men do bad things to my sister."

"The girl is your sister?"

The Paiute nodded, his eyes holding on Drake's face. "You know they got Henie, huh?"

"I know."

"They got spare horse. It yours?"

"Yes, it's mine."

"You follow them to get horse?"

"I follow them to try to get back your sister."

"You been beat up too, I see. By them?"

"When I tried to help her."

The Paiute dismounted, walked to Drake, and handed him the reins.

"You ride a while, I walk. My name it's Tagee. We both after same thing. We go together. All right?"

Drake hesitated a moment, then handed him his carbine, took the reins, and mounted.

"All right," he said.

CHAPTER 5

THEY BROKE OUT of the rolling country onto a flat plain, and a couple of miles ahead they saw the next swing station.

As they drew near, Drake noted its similarity to the other.

Here, however, only one tender appeared, although there was the sound of someone hammering iron in the area of the stables.

When they reached the station structure, the tender said to Drake, "Two men and one horse—no way to cross this desert."

Drake had no inclination to repeat the conversation he'd had at the previous station.

He did ask if a horse was available and received a like answer to his earlier question, including mention of the spare one being led by three rough customers who had stopped for water.

"And an Injun girl," the tender said. He looked at Tagee who stood next to the still-mounted Drake. "Tied up."

"You ask why?" Drake said.

"None of my business," the station keeper said. "Not when she was only an Injun." He paused. "This one with you, he your guide or something?"

"My partner," Drake said.

"Where you trying to get?"

"Antelope Wells."

"Well, water your horse, fill the canteens, and you'll make it. Ain't much over a dozen miles."

29

They set off again, Tagee motioning Drake into the saddle once more.

Walking beside him, Tagee said after a while, "You damn good shot with guns, huh? I hear how you can shoot, in Goldfield."

Drake said nothing.

"Me," Tagee said. "I don't shoot so good. But I kill badmen when we catch up."

Drake was still silent.

"I miss," Tagee said, "you shoot, huh?" When Drake didn't answer, he said, "They got to die for what they done to Henie."

"The important thing," Drake said, "is to get her away from them."

The Paiute scowled. "You know what I say? They got to die too."

"I'm not a killer," Drake said. He felt the Paiute's eyes looking up at him.

He met Tagee's eyes, saw the harsh irony in them, and dreaded that Tagee would make reference to what had happened to Molly.

When Tagee said nothing, he said, "We'll do what has to be done."

And sensed it wasn't enough to satisfy the Indian.

They continued on, a strained silence between them until Tagee said, "It time for me to ride my horse."

Drake halted and slipped from the saddle and held out the reins.

Tagee took them roughly and mounted.

A long time later he said, "Why you bother about my sister?"

"I told you," Drake said. "She came to me for help, and I tried but couldn't give it to her."

"That all?"

"No, not all. I was driven by the treatment they were giving her. It bothered me to see that."

"It bother you?"

"I do not like to see a woman hurt," Drake said, and again he felt Tagee's stare upon him. He did not look up.

After a pause, Tagee said, "All right. I believe it."

He did not speak again for a long period.

So long that Drake glanced up at him and saw a lingering frown on his face.

At that moment Tagee looked down and his frown deepened.

He said, "My sister, you see how pretty she been?"

Drake hesitated, then said, "Her face was beaten. Why do you ask?"

The Indian's face grew still harder.

"She pretty, all right. I see many white men make eyes at Henie. White men, they want the one thing from her. They make sweet talk when she work in hotel, offer to give her better job with them. But she don't been fooled."

"I understand."

"You understand? You understand I kill any man if he ever hurt her?"

Looking at him, Drake could believe it. He nodded.

"Any man," Tagee said. "Even you."

Drake felt rising anger, but he said nothing. It was clear to him the young Paiute had strong protective feelings for his sister. He could make allowances for that.

They approached what Drake judged must be Antelope Wells.

The name reminded him of his repeated contact with the antelope doe at Tawich, and he quickly shoved the memory from his mind. It was possible he would find their quarry in the struggling mining town, and he had better be ready for the confrontation.

The settlement was small, with a cluster of shacks weathered by two or three years. There were mine-shaft head frames scattered about, the tailings moderate. A place of uncertain prospects, like many another in Nevada.

But it was a land where uncertainty never seemed to

daunt the hopeful, as evidenced by the mercantile store, small hotel, stage station and livery, and saloon. It was a land of taking chances, Drake thought.

As he and Tagee might well be about to do.

He walked to the hitch rack in front of the saloon. "I'll go in and make inquiries," he said.

"If they in there, you be one against three. I go with you."

"Indians not allowed in a saloon. Besides, their horses aren't here."

"They maybe been here couple days. Horses in livery."

"I'll find out," Drake said.

He moved toward the saloon doors and entered.

It was not yet evening, and only a couple of men in work clothes sat drinking at a corner table.

From behind the bar a tender watched his entry. His eyes appraised Drake's weapons, and his face turned expressionless.

But he said, "You on a bear hunt, friend?"

Drake ignored the remark. "I'll take a beer."

"Sure." The barkeep drew one, set it in front of him, and glanced out through a dusty window.

Tagee had dismounted and tied the horse to the hitch rack.

He stood beside it in a posture of alertness, holding in one hand his carbine, his eyes focused on the saloon entrance.

The barkeep looked back at Drake. "I seen you come up with the Injun out there. Him riding, and you walking. No wonder you look thirsty. Must be a good friend."

Drake gave a short nod but said nothing.

"Him standing there with that gun at the ready—maybe you was expecting trouble when you walked in?"

"It's possible."

"But it ain't here, so you can enjoy your beer."

Drake decided it was time for his own questions. "You seen three rough customers, one a big man?"

"You a lawman?"

"You see a badge?"

The barkeep looked out of the window again at Tagee, then said, "They had a hands-tied squaw with them, and though it was morning and I had no customers yet, they brought her in, too, and I objected. I don't let no Injuns in my place." He nodded toward the street. "Him out there might have something to do with her, maybe?"

"Maybe."

"Well, they shoved her into a chair and ordered beer and whiskey chasers and sat there drinking their fill. After a couple of rounds, I asked if they wanted something for the girl, and the big one said, 'Hell, man, don't you know that would be against the law to serve alcohol to an Injun?' And they all laughed."

"How did the girl look?" Drake said.

"A good-looking young Injun girl, but bad used. Hell, she looked so beat, I'd have brought her a beer, Injun or not, had they been willing to pay for it."

"Generous of you," Drake said dryly.

"I been called bighearted sometimes."

"After they drank their fill, did they ride on out?"

"They sure as hell did. And the sons-of-bitches never paid for what they drank, neither."

"Didn't you object?"

"Yeah, I did. Until the big one pulled his gun as I was about to reach for the sawed-off Greener I keep behind the bar here. Hell, money don't mean that much to me."

"I'll need a horse," Drake said.

"You going after them?"

"That's my intention."

"You good with them guns?"

Drake hesitated, then said, "I was once."

"I hope to hell you still are, if you catch up with them."

"Yeah."

"You got money, you ought to get a fair horse at the livery."

"Thanks for the information."

"You catch up, kill the bastards . . ."

Drake gave him a studying look. Perhaps the barkeep had been more bothered by their rough treatment of the girl than he let on.

". . . they deserve it for not paying for the drinks."

Together, Drake and Tagee walked down the street, the Paiute leading his mount.

The livery was located at the stage station, but with a separate access. A man with a blacksmith's build waited as they neared. As they came up, he said to Drake, "Seen you coming when I looked out. Seen you maybe needed a horse."

"Have you got one to sell?"

"I keep them to rent. But I got one I maybe could let you have for a price."

"Let's see it."

"Tie yours up and have a look." He led the way down between stalls and stopped outside one of them. "This one," he said.

Drake studied the mount. "Looks hard ridden."

Tagee, standing beside him staring, said, "I know that horse."

"How?" Drake said.

"One my sister been ride."

The liveryman said, "That was your sister with them hardcases?"

"It hers."

"You sure?"

"This horse," Tagee said, "it got founder of left front hoof."

"Well, it was a situation there I didn't like," the ostler said. "So I won't lie to you. They had a spare horse with them and traded this one for forage and grain for the others. I could see this one had come up lame, and wasn't too willing about the trade, but they said take it or leave it. Well, hell, I figured I could unload it on somebody and didn't have no choice, so I took it." He paused. "What I know now, I wouldn't try to con you boys even if I could."

Drake said, "That spare horse they had was stolen from me."

"Another reason to be after them. But me personal, I'd not tangle with them for that. They was cut rough, you want my opinion."

"What about a horse for me?"

"Can you pay?"

"A reasonable price, yes."

"A few to pick from, back in the corral."

A half-dozen animals were in the enclosure.

The ostler said, "That bay gelding would be a good choice for you. And I'm telling you true because I want you to get that girl free."

Drake gave him a curious look. "I'm surprised you care, her being Indian."

"Not all of us think alike, comes to Injuns."

"Seems like most do," Drake said.

"Them hardcases," the liveryman said, "why do you suppose they keep that girl with them?"

"Can't you guess?"

"They had her lot of days," Tagee said. "I think do bad things to her."

"By god, they must be as hard up as a bunch of convicts. Say! A freighter, come in from Beatty few days back, said he'd heard there about a breakout at the Carson prison. Lawmen had been rounding up escapees along the California line. Maybe these three was ones come this way instead."

The idea caught Drake's interest and he considered it briefly.

Then he said, "Might account for their abuse of her."

"The bastards," the liveryman said. "I hope you catch up and kill the sons-of-bitches."

CHAPTER 6

THE TROUBLE BETWEEN Jack Shaw and his partners began when they lost the trace they were following twenty miles southeast of the Wells. At one time it had led to Indian Springs, Shaw insisted to the others.

"Dammit!" he said, "I took this trail six years ago. Looks like it ain't been used maybe since."

"Thickest damn growth of creosote, cactus, and Joshuas I ever seen," Huff said.

"What you going to do now?" Longo said.

"We'll keep on going the same direction. Maybe run onto another stretch of it further on."

Longo said, "And damn well maybe we won't. Like looking for a needle in a manure pile."

"Where and what is Indian Springs?" Huff said.

"Springs is near the far side of this desert. And not too far beyond is the Arizona line."

"You going to guess your way there?" Longo said.

"I know the general direction."

It irritated Shaw when the other two were silent.

"Listen, you bastards, I got you clear away from that prison hellhole. You want to take off on your own now, go ahead."

"Where?" Longo said. "Neither one of us ever been in these parts before."

"You don't have much choice then, do you."

There was another silence, and this time Shaw gave them a hard grin. He kicked his horse and moved on.

A while later Longo moved up beside him. "You know of any waterholes on the way ahead?"

"There's a couple."

"But without a trail, you could damn well miss them."

Shaw made no comment.

Long then said, "That Injun wench's been sharing our water."

"She's got to live."

"Why? Me and Huff got our needs satisfied. We ain't got no more use for her, or ain't you noticed?"

"I noticed. And that's the way I want it from now on."

"I say turn her loose. Save us some water that way. She can make it back to that last stop we was at."

Shaw did not speak for a long moment. Then he said, "One thing wrong with what you're saying. I ain't through with her myself."

"I ain't seen you rolling her in the sand anymore."

"A man's feelings toward a woman can change," Shaw said.

"What the hell are you saying?"

"She means something to me, is all. Like I said, I don't want you or Huff using her again."

"Well, well," Longo said. "If you wasn't saying it, I wouldn't believe it."

Huff had drawn up on the other side of Shaw to listen, and now he said, "Me neither, by god. Kind of beats all, don't it? Nearest thing I ever heard that comes close to it is how some men fell in love with whores and married them."

"It ain't like you, Shaw."

"Maybe so," Shaw said. "But I'm telling you how it is. The girl stays with us. And you both keep your hands off her."

Longo said, "I've seen the way she scowls at you. What you're saying has got to be one-sided. You figure you can change that?"

Shaw didn't answer him. But he frowned.

*   *   *

Shaw looked at her more often now. The days on the desert had not visibly exhausted her, and this was a thing he had come to admire. Only an Indian woman could endure the roughness of it and not show the signs.

He had not made a decision on what he would do when he reached Arizona. Would he try to go straight and keep out of trouble? Or return to outlawry? It depended on the way the chips fell, he guessed, and left it in his mind that way.

But she satisfied his physical needs and was tough enough to ride the trail with him whatever that turned out to be.

He had never been gentle with women, knowing only whores.

And he had used the Indian girl as one. But the fact that she resisted him each time had strangely earned his respect.

So much that when he had last taken her, a night or two before, he had felt a certain amount of remorse afterward.

It was a new feeling for him, and he even felt sorry that he had beat her there in that ghost town when she had gone to that prospector for help.

He was determined now to make it up to her. When they reached Arizona, he would keep her with him, if he could.

Take care of her. For a while, at least.

Those were his thoughts.

He removed the remaining knots that lashed her hands to her saddle horn, giving her free rein as a gesture of his changed attitude toward her.

She accepted his action with no show of response.

It irritated him that she spoke no thanks, but he fought that down, realizing it was going to take time to bring her around.

He forced a smile, but her face remained expressionless in silent rebuke.

"It'll make it a little easier on you," he said.

She said nothing.

"I'm sorry for the rough treatment."

She simply met his eyes with a cold stare.

"Goddammit! Can't you talk?"

"Yes," she said. "You are a pig."

He took that remark in silence, surprised that he had no desire to hit her.

Instead he said, "I want things to be different between us from now on."

"Why?"

He shrugged. "I don't know. I just do."

Her hard stare turned thoughtful.

He saw this and said, "You think about what I'm saying, you hear?"

"I hear," she said. "You are a strange man."

"Maybe so. But I never felt like this before. Not since maybe when I was real young."

She did not speak again, but she let her face soften slightly.

He saw that and seemed pleased.

He turned away then and rode on a little ahead to where Huff and Longo were riding.

Longo said, "I seen you undo them ties on the Injun."

"So what?"

"You getting soft, Shaw?"

Shaw scowled. "You think so, try me."

Longo made no further comment.

The day grew hotter. By midafternoon, Shaw called a halt as they reached a low plateau heavily dotted with the spiny-leaved Joshua trees, crooked limbs upraised as if threatening the blazing yellow sky.

"Not much shade," he said. "But it's all there is. Pick a tree, each of you, and we'll take a short break."

Though thicker than usual, the grotesque trees were still yards apart at the closest. Each tied his mount to a bush nearest his selected tree.

Shaw waited until the Paiute girl had tied her horse as far from the others as she could get. He then found himself a spot twenty yards away, nearest to her.

Soon they were all sprawled in the meager protection of the Joshuas.

Shaw awoke from a short sleep, cursing himself, a sense of trouble goading him. His eyes went instantly to where the girl had been. He knew before they reached there that she was gone!

He got to his feet, his glance swinging about the landscape, searching for sight of her.

He looked then at where Longo and Huff lay. Both seemed asleep. He unhitched his horse and got into the saddle.

From that slightly higher vantage he again quickly viewed the surroundings. They were empty.

He rode over to the others and called, "Get up! Get up!"

Longo rolled over and looked up at him.

"What the hell's the matter?"

"The girl is gone."

"Good!" Longo said.

Huff stirred at the sound and looked at him, then up at Shaw, and said, "What the hell?"

Shaw said again, "The girl is gone."

Huff sat up but said nothing.

"Get mounted!"

"Why?" Longo said. "Best damn thing could have happened."

"Get on your horse, goddammit!"

"Why, sure," Longo said, getting up. "Anything you say, Shaw."

Huff got up, too.

Minutes later they were in their saddles.

"Where to?" Longo said.

"Either one of you see her leave?"

"I didn't," Huff said.

Shaw looked at Longo. "You?"

"I must have been sound asleep."

Shaw scrutinized him sharply.

Longo said, "Why you staring at me? I'm telling you true." He paused. "But I'll tell this too, if I'd seen her leave I wouldn't have told you. Good riddance, I say."

"Listen, you! You want to be led out of this desert, you help to get her back. Now spread out over by where she was resting and look for her tracks."

Shaw rode over to where she had been, trailed by Huff.

Longo hesitated until Shaw looked back over his shoulder at him. Then he followed.

The girl had been surprised when the one called Shaw did not bind her ankles when they stopped to rest. It had something to do with what he had talked about earlier, she supposed, although she was not certain what that was all about, either.

Perhaps he had not deemed it necessary to tie her, counting only on a short period of recuperation.

And not counting on them all falling asleep except her. No, not all of them, maybe. She had looked over and seen the argumentative one stirring as if awake. She had partly overheard their conflicting discussion of her while they were riding, and though not at all sure, she did not expect trouble from that one.

It was easy then. She simply arose, untied her horse, mounted, and rode away.

Despite the heat she pushed the horse at first, hoping to gain some ground before Shaw awoke.

She had started thoughtlessly to retrace their tracks back to the place where they had traded her limping mount for the one she now rode.

That was one advantage she had, she thought. This new horse was fresh, unlike those of the men, which had been ridden for days.

She came to a stretch of trail where the ground was harder. So hard that even their recent passing had left no tracks. Here, too, there was a stretch to the northeast of thick creosote bush that appeared almost impenetrable.

She did not hesitate. She turned the gelding, and though it balked at first, she urged it into the heavy growth.

The convicts followed her trail until it disappeared on the hard earth. But they recalled passing that way previously and continued on until they picked up their own prints again.

"Must be headed back the same way we come," Huff said.

None of them were expert trackers, and it wasn't until they came to a stretch of soft sand that Shaw pulled up, swearing.

Longo had a faint smirk on his face as he said, "What's up?"

"No hoofprints going up the trail—just ours coming down."

"I wondered how long it'd take you to notice."

"You knew?" Shaw said.

"A short ways back."

"You son of a bitch!"

"I wanted to give her a chance to get herself real lost," Longo said. "I told you how I feel."

"I should have left you back in Carson City," Shaw said.

"The only difference we got is about the girl."

"It's enough."

Shaw turned his mount and started back. "Look for where she turned off," he said to Huff.

As if to make amends, Longo said, "It must have been back in that dense brush we went by."

"Keep looking all the way back," Shaw said. "*Both* of you!"

It was Shaw who found the spot. The horse had slightly parted the branches of the creosote, tough as it was.

Longo said, "We going to beat ourself though that stuff?"

"She did it."

"I ain't no Injun."

"She's a woman," Shaw said. "If she did it, we can."

"She had a reason."

"So do I," Shaw said. "I ain't leaving this desert until I find her."

"And if I don't join your hunt?"

"Try finding your way out of this desert alone," Shaw said, forcing his reluctant mount into the heavy brush.

Huff pushed in behind him.

Longo sat in his saddle, unmoving, for a long moment, then uttered a curse and followed.

It was tough going, the bushes raking at their legs and at the bodies of the horses.

"How far in front they are, you think?" Tagee said to Drake.

"Half day maybe. They wasted time at the Wells."

"Half day, maybe ten mile?" Tagee said. "How we going catch them?"

Drake shrugged. "We can only keep on trying. Hope something slows them."

"We need go faster to catch them."

"In this heat we'll kill the horses."

"That true."

They rode on in silence.

The expanse of heavy creosote bush was on rolling terrain, and the convicts' view was limited. There was no sign of the girl; only an occasional broken branch marked the route she had taken.

The going was slow and hard, and somewhere deep into the growth they lost even these meager markings.

Shaw, in the lead, halted.

Longo and Huff, in single file behind him, stopped. Longo said, "You lost?"

Shaw did not answer. Instead, he sat in deep thought. Finally he said, "I can only think that she tried to confuse us. And once in this damned jungle of bushes got lost herself."

"So?"

"Without water, she'd realize the only way to go is to the Wells, which is where she started for. She must have figured to gain a lead by losing us awhile in here."

"Damn fool Injun," Longo said.

"Not so dumb," Huff said. "She done what she figured."

Shaw said, "We'll head north until we break out of this tangle. The Wells is northwest from where we started. We ought to intersect it that way."

Longo said, "We lost a lot of time following her in here."

"So did she," Shaw said. He paused, "But at least she tried."

Longo gave him an odd look. "You complimenting her for that?"

"Just stating a fact," Shaw said, and began pushing his horse northward.

The girl kept pushing west, hoping to break out, but the thick growth seemed to go on endlessly. She was not an accomplished horsewoman, and the balky behavior of her mount made for exhausting progress.

Her only familiarity with this part of the desert was the trail on which she had been led by her captors. If she could reach the town without being apprehended, she hoped to beg a canteen of water from the liverymen—perhaps even grain for the horse. He had seemed somewhat concerned about her treatment at their hands, even if he had been reluctant to object. She would then retrace the way back to the ghost town where that lone white man had tried to help her.

She had gathered from overheard bits of conversations that her captors were escaped convicts seeking to leave Nevada. This gave her hope that they would not delay their flight in any prolonged search for her.

So still deep in the heavy growth of creosote, she finally turned toward where she judged that place they called Antelope Wells was.

Tagee said to Drake, "Look south. You see some dust maybe?"

Drake squinted against the reflected glare of the sun.

"Yes, I see it."

It was considerably west of the way they were headed. Behind it was a darkened background that he guessed was an expanse of heavy foliage.

"Those somebody," Tagee said, "maybe they can tell where are them we been after."

"Maybe," Drake said. He looked about him on either side. To the left was a rocky ledge on a terrain of knolls. "We best take cover over there until we find out."

Tagee gave him a sharp look. "You think maybe they bad ones? I don't think so. Because if so, they don't come this way."

Drake didn't argue. He was already turning his horse toward the hillocks.

After a moment, Tagee followed.

The rock outthrust was high enough to shield them from sight.

Once there they waited. It seemed the riders were coming directly toward them.

Tagee said, "Maybe they seen us."

"I doubt it," Drake said. "We weren't kicking up any dust here."

Tagee had slipped his carbine from its saddle scabbard and was holding it in his hands. It was a Krag-Jorgensen 30-40, with a scarred stock that showed careless usage.

"Do you have bullets?" Drake said.

"Five in the gun," the Paiute said. "That all it hold."

"You took after the bad ones with only five shots?"

"It is all I had."

"You must be a good shot," Drake said.

"No. I told you no."

"All right," Drake said. He nodded toward his own weapon still on his horse. "Mine uses the same caliber. I've got extra ammo in a pouch. Eighteen ninety-five model Winchester."

"Get it!"

"Bullets? Sure." Drake moved toward his horse.

"Your gun too," Tagee said. "What you wait for?"

Drake did not answer him. He came back with his weapon in one hand, a medium-sized sack of bullets in the other.

The Paiute eyed him curiously, then said, "You better give me handful them bullets."

Drake handed him the sack.

Tagee took out enough for a couple of magazine re-loads.

"You got full load?" he said, giving Drake a close look again.

"I wouldn't be carrying an empty weapon."

"All right," Tagee said. "But sometime I wonder."

"What does that mean?"

The Paiute shrugged. "I don't know."

The convicts came close enough to be recognized by Drake.

"That's them," he said.

"We let them get closer, huh?" Tagee said. "You shoot first, say when."

They waited, carbines ready, as the horsemen came into effective firing range. Still Drake did not shoot.

At that moment a rattlesnake emerged from a crevice in the ledge behind which Drake's mount was ground-tethered.

The horse shrieked and bolted up the hillside into view of the approaching riders.

They halted and reached for their rifles.

Tagee fired.

The convicts responded with a fusillade of bullets that ricocheted off the ledge.

One whined off and stung the horse that had paused above. It sounded its pain, and Tagee turned and saw it start to move off.

He said to Drake, "You give me cover fire. I go to get horse."

Without waiting for an answer, he started running up the slope.

And became the target for the shooters.

The girl had broken out of the creosote cover only a short distance west of the convicts' position.

Almost at once she took in the battle scene, recognized the horse as her brother's, recognized Tagee as he rushed toward it. And saw the puffs of dust kicked up by the bullets striking near him.

All thought of escape left her. She drove heels to her tired mount and got it into a trot, screaming at the convicts to draw their attention.

As one, the three turned.

They stared as she came, momentarily forgetting their attack.

Their abrupt cease-fire gave Tagee time to reach the horse and pull it back to the ledge's cover.

Behind the ledge, Drake, who had been firing near-misses at the convicts, stopped also.

He watched in dismay as the girl rode up deliberately to her captors.

Tagee, seeing him doing nothing, said, "No shooting now? You kill them all?"

"I stopped when your sister joined them."

The Paiute looked down.

The biggest of the men had grabbed the reins out of the girl's hands and was leading her fast away, the other two close behind them.

"You don't kill none?" Tagee said.

Drake did not answer at first. Then he said, "I was afraid of hitting your sister."

"She was close to them?"

"You can see that now."

"Now, yes."

Drake was silent, then said, "I killed my own woman, shooting at a target too close to her."

The Paiute said nothing.

But he shook his head.

As they rode southward, Longo pulled alongside Shaw.

He said, "Why the hell did this squaw come back to us?"

"Ask her," Shaw said. "I'd like to know myself."

"Hell, she never would talk to me."

"Me, neither. Right now, I'm only interested in getting away from them bushwhackers."

"I figure they was only two," Longo said.

"Two behind that ledge," Shaw said. "Would you want to charge against that?"

"Hell, no!"

"If they're after us," Shaw said, "we'll pick a better spot for a showdown."

"The one done most of the shooting had us in the open, and he still missed every shot," Longo said. "He must be a godawful lousy shot."

CHAPTER 7

EVENTUALLY THEY GOT back to where they had been before the girl ran off from them. They paused there for a rest, but this time Shaw kept her in bonds after she had a relief break.

And none of them fell asleep; they stayed bunched together.

Longo said to Shaw, "Well, ask her."

Shaw was griped by Longo's insistence. He said, "Why she ran off?"

"Hell, no! Why she come back to us."

"I'll ask her later. In private."

"Last time you talked to her private, she got away."

Shaw looked over at her and saw she was listening, expressionless.

Longo said, "Listen, Shaw, we're in this together. And I want to know. It don't make sense she'd get free, then come back that way."

Shaw spoke gently to her. "You heard the question, girl. Tell him why."

She was silent.

Longo said, "Listen, you Injun slut, talk!"

She said then, "I had no water. I got lost in the brush, and I knew I would need water to go on."

"A likely story," Longo said.

"I knew then I was better off with you," she said to Shaw.

He nodded. "Makes sense."

"Bull!" Longo said.

"She's had it tough these past few days," Shaw said. "She got confused out there alone."

49

"Shaw, for cripes sake, she's a Paiute! Desert ain't nothing strange to her."

"She ain't no blanket Injun. You can tell that the way she talks," Shaw said.

"She must have seen we was being shot at. It was a chance for her to escape."

Shaw's eyes met hers. "How about what he's saying?"

"I was confused," she said.

"I don't believe her," Longo said.

"Let her rest for now," Shaw said. "I'll talk to her later."

Longo wouldn't let it drop. He turned to the girl and said, "Did you see them that was shooting at us?"

She shook her head. "They were hidden, weren't they?"

"*But shooting at us.* You wanted to get away from us—didn't you figure that might help you?"

"I see now I made a mistake," she said. Then, in a rising voice of self-accusation, she added, "I was a fool."

Huff spoke up then for the first time. "Hell, Longo, you know the dumb things that Injuns do sometimes."

"Well," Longo said, "that's a true fact, for sure."

Shaw said, "Mount up. Somewhere up ahead there's a lava bed east of a dark mountain. We reach that, we'll find plenty of protection to make a stand against them shooters, if they follow."

Huff said, "Why would they be on our trail?"

Shaw said, "Bounty hunters maybe. Could be a reward on us. Somebody might have got wise after seeing us leave Tonopah, then hearing about bounty money."

Huff said, "Let's go then. Being caught in the open like we was don't appeal none to me."

"What about the squaw?" Longo said to Shaw. "You going to tie her up?"

"She knows now she can't reach water alone."

"We're almost out our own self."

"There's a spring near that lava bed," Shaw said.

"I hope to hell you can find it," Huff said.

*   *   *

The girl was relieved that her surrender had saved her brother from being killed, and she was determined not to reveal his identity. She had been astounded to see him above the ledge, struggling with his spooked horse. He must have set out to find her when she failed to visit him.

But who was it with him, the one firing at the convicts? Who could Tagee have brought with him? No one would help them, but then she thought of the man at the ghost town. He had tried to shield her from Shaw, until he was beaten unconscious.

For the first time she felt an awakening of hope, because her brother and his friend were nearby and trying to rescue her. If there were only the two of them against the three armed convicts, she felt great concern about their chances of success.

What could she do to help them?

She thought then of the big man, Shaw. His apparent change of feeling toward her seemed surprisingly genuine. She sensed this made him somewhat vulnerable. He was a hard man, not familiar with the ways of women, she thought.

Could she use this to help solve her predicament?

Shaw was intent now on finding the lava field where he recalled there was a spring.

Still his mind kept returning to the girl.

He only half-believed her story of being confused by the gunfire and could understand Longo's doubting it. The difference was he *wanted* to believe her.

He wanted to even believe she had returned because of him. But he had his own strong doubts about that.

Well, even if he had not won her affections yet, he would, he thought. He'd have to make more amends than just untying her bonds. He'd have to do something to show her he had come to care.

The emotions he was feeling were new to his experience, at least in many years, and he was uncertain what they were. Hell, he was forty years old—had she awakened long-dormant emotions from his youth?

Goddammit! He was Jack Shaw, outlaw and prison-hardened escaped life-term convict. How could he feel this way?

Was her close presence, after his years of being without, wreaking this effect?

Or was it something deeper than that?

Longo interrupted his thinking.

"That black-looking mountain peak showing ahead, a little to our right, is that what you're looking for?"

"That's it," Shaw said. "That might've been what spewed out the lava a long time ago. As I remember, the spring is near the east edge of the lava spread. If so, we're headed right to it."

"About time," Longo said. "Our canteens are near empty." He paused, then said, "You think them two bushwhackers are still on our trail?"

"You can count on it," Shaw said. "When we reach the spring, we'll hole up among the lava rocks and do some ambushing of our own."

"They get in among that lava they'll maybe have cover their own self," Huff said.

"I don't figure to let them in," Shaw said. "That's the whole idea."

"We ain't there yet," Longo said.

The girl was listening, wondering what she could do to prevent her brother from riding into a trap. There was nothing she could do now, she thought. She'd have to think of something by the time they reached the lava.

Soon they came upon it, beyond a rise in the tableland. A devil's mix of fixed molten lava shapes with boulder-sized pieces strewn between.

As they entered it, Longo looked back at the higher ground they had just descended. He swore and said, "If them bastards are closing in, we won't see them till they're almost on us."

"Works both ways," Shaw said. "They'll be within rifle shot before they cross the skyline there."

"Where's that spring you talked about?"

"Farther in, as I remember."

"We need water."

"We'll have to wait. We'll stay right here behind these lava piles. Fight thirsty, goddammit! Catch them as they start down toward us."

"What about the squaw there?" Longo said.

"What about her?"

"You forgetting she tried to get away once? I ain't. Them bastards may be a couple of lawmen. I'm thinking she'd damn rather be with them than us, that's for sure . . . even if they're bounty hunters." He paused. "I wish to hell she *would* get away, but I don't want her warning them we're here waiting."

Shaw was silent.

"Shaw, you either tie her up and gag her, too, or you'll be here fighting alone."

"That's right," Huff said.

"And put her back there someplace where she can't wiggle around and show herself," Longo said.

"I reckon you're right," Shaw said. They were dismounted now, and he took the girl by the arm and led her back to where she was well shielded. He began to tie her up with the thongs he had pocketed.

"Please," she said then. "Not too tight. They hurt when they are tight."

"I don't want to hurt you," he said.

"I know you don't," she said.

He showed surprise. "I'm glad. It makes me feel good that you're starting to trust me."

"Please, then. Not too tight."

"I won't," he said.

"And no gag, please, Shaw."

He hesitated, then said, "I've got to."

"Please, not too tight. I can hardly breathe if it's too tight."

"All right," he said.

Before he could put the neckerchief gag in her mouth, she said, "Why are those men after you?"

He was silent, then said, "Bounty hunters, I think."

"Bounty hunters?"

Again he did not answer at once. Then he said, "You have overheard us talking. You must know by now that we're escaped from the prison. There could well be a bounty on our heads."

"Why were you in prison?"

"It's a long story," he said. "I got off on the wrong foot when I was young."

"Why did you break out of prison?"

"They had given me an unfair sentence—for life. I had done five years of it, but they were never going to let me out. I had been an outlaw, I admit that. But five years was enough punishment." He paused. "If we get free of them bounty men, I'm going to Arizona to start over. Free from the outlaw trail." He looked at her earnestly and said, "I want you to stay with me. I want you to be with me when I go straight."

"But if you kill those lawmen?"

"They're not lawmen. They won't try to arrest us. Killing is their way to get a reward. Most of them are no better than outlaws themselves. We will be shooting them in self-defense."

"There must be another way."

"Trust me," he said. "There isn't."

"I do trust you," she said, "but if you trusted me, you wouldn't gag me."

He seemed to be wavering, and that gave her hope.

At that moment Longo's voice sounded from a few feet away.

"What the hell you doing, Shaw? Get the job done on her and get back to our posts. Them bastards may be coming over that hill any time now!"

Shaw met the girl's eyes and shook his head. But she could feel he was careful not to tighten the gag enough to interfere with her breathing.

Despite her pleading, he left her hidden behind a large chunk of lava, bound hand and foot, as he and Longo hurried away to join Huff and wait for the expected approach of their pursuers.

Henie was terrified for her brother and the other man. They were riding into a trap and there was nothing she could do to warn them.

Tagee said, "You got water?"

"A little left. You?"

"Same. Better be some soon."

Drake said, "I think those convicts must need it, too. At least one of them must know something about this desert, or they wouldn't have taken this route. Must know of some possible waterholes."

"Better be," the Paiute said. "I never been this desert before."

"I heard that your people can find water out here where a white man can't."

"Sometimes, maybe. But if there no water where we dig, we don't find either. Besides, I been live like white long time now. Forget many Paiute things."

"That black mountain peak we see above that low hill ahead," Drake said, "might have a spring nearby."

"Maybe so. Them badmen went over the hill, looks like. Maybe we find out something on other side."

Drake was silent, thinking about that. The convicts must

be almost certain they were still being followed. He had been half-expecting an attack from the brush cover along the way ever since he'd lost sight of them as they sped away with the girl.

When he and Tagee reached the top of that hill they could be open targets.

"Hold up a minute!" he said. "We're not going to follow their tracks up that climb."

"We don't, we lose them."

Drake gestured to either side. The hill was only one of an extended low range.

"We'll swing wide of it ."

"We lose time."

"Lose time," Drake said, "but maybe save lives."

Tagee was thoughtful. "All right. Which way we go?"

Drake pointed to the west.

"Looks like there might be a pass, a mile or so that way."

They turned and rode in that direction.

The convicts were ready and waiting, hidden behind the weird-shaped lava castings.

As time passed, Shaw began to have second thoughts about their position.

"How long we got to wait?" Longo said. "These volcanic clumps are hotter than hell in this sun. And I already drank up my water."

"Like I said before," Shaw said, "fight thirsty."

"The hell! I got the notion to go find that spring for myself."

"Think you can?"

"I ain't so sure *you* can," Longo said.

"I got a lot better chance than you have. I've been there before."

"It's the waiting that gets me," Longo said. "We ain't even sure them bounty men are going to come over that rise."

This was so close to Shaw's own thinking that he made no reply.

"You hear what I'm saying?"

"We'll stay put a while longer."

"I hope to hell you know what you're doing," Longo said. His eyes went to the brow of the rise again, as did those of Shaw.

Shaw said, "I know, goddammit!" But even as he said it, he glanced both east and west along the hill range. Depending on how smart the bounty men were, he thought, they could cross anywhere.

So what could he do about it? With three men, there was no way he could cover all the possibilities.

The alternative was to take the trail again, keep on the run. But he had decided the lava field was the place to make a stand. And here he would stay.

No matter where the bastards crossed, they'd still have to seek him and his partners out among the basaltic heaps. And with three against two, the odds would be in Shaw's favor.

He said then, "Huff, you keep watching the top of the rise there. Longo, you keep a scan on the west. I'll watch to the east for any sign of them."

Each man watched as instructed.

Twice though, Shaw glanced at Longo and the second time found that his gaze had wandered back to the rise.

"Dammit!" Shaw said. "I told you to watch the west."

"I been doing it."

"Like hell!"

"I only looked away for a minute."

"That's all it could take to miss them!"

"I wanted to make sure Huff was watching above there."

"Mind your own job," Shaw said.

There were times when he thought he'd made a mistake taking Longo with him when they broke out. But you never really knew a man until you'd taken the trail with him.

He wouldn't want him or Huff along after they reached Arizona. He'd only want the girl from then on. Now, thinking of her, he wondered how she was enduring being tied back there, alone in the heat.

He was bothered by the thought and tried to shove it from his mind. But he kept seeing her there as he had left her, and hoping he'd not gagged her too tightly.

When they got across into Arizona, he thought, he would treat her much better.

At that moment Longo cried out. "There!"

Shaw looked and glimpsed the two riders just as they disappeared into the lava field a couple of miles to the west.

CHAPTER 8

TAGEE SAID, "HOW we find them now?"

"Work our way toward them," Drake said, "along the edge of that lava."

"Maybe they don't even be there. Maybe they just keep going south. Maybe we just been lose more time."

"It was a chance we took."

"Chance *you* took," Tagee said. "I begin think you don't want to find."

Drake did not comment on the implication. It bothered him every time Tagee said something like that, mainly because Drake was not sure Tagee was wrong about him.

But now Drake was going to find out whether the Paiute's suspicions were right. He was about to find out for sure why he had missed the convicts back there when he fired at them from the ledge.

Because he was out of practice with a rifle?

Because he was afraid of hitting the girl?

Or because he could not bring himself to wound or kill anyone, even to save Henie?

Now he was going to finally know. He felt dead certain that those three convicts were waiting there in that lava bed to kill him. Him and Tagee. Unless he killed them first.

"Well?" Tagee said.

Still not speaking, Drake entered the field and began threading his way through the volcanic shapes toward where he expected the enemy to be.

Longo said, "They came into the field, same as us. But there's no telling where they'll be."

"It's us they're after," Shaw said. "We can stay here and wait."

"They may stumble onto the Injun squaw," Longo said. "Not that I care." He paused. "Or did you forget about her?"

"We'll move over to where she is. If they find her, they'll find us ready for them."

"Let's get on with it then. Give ourself time to pick good positions."

"I'm for that," Huff said.

Shaw led the way toward where they'd left her. He stopped when he got there.

Huff said, "Them bounty men must have already come and freed her!"

"Couldn't have," Longo said. "A few minutes ago they were a mile or more away."

He walked over a few paces and picked up a cloth from the ground.

He brought it back and handed it to Shaw. "Your neckerchief, ain't it? The one you used to gag her with?"

Shaw took it and stuffed it in his pocket, not saying a word. He was feeling rage, but disappointment too.

Longo said, "I heard her begging you not to tie her up too tight. It looks like you were listening."

"Not intentional," Shaw said.

"You let that squaw make a fool out of you," Longo said.

"If she meets up with them bastards," Huff said, "she could lead them back here to us."

"So?" Shaw said. "That's what we want, ain't it?"

"I guess so. Let's get forted up."

"Spread out some," Shaw said, "and pick your cover."

Then, as they moved away from him he called, "Listen both of you—when them bullets get to flying, if the girl is with them, take care neither of you hit her."

"Yeah, Shaw," Huff said.

Longo nodded, but he grinned.

          *   *   *

Now moving eastward, Tagee said, "Wait! I hear something."

Drake stopped, listening.

"I don't hear anything."

"I think maybe you practice shoot gun too much. Bullet noise make you deaf."

"Well, what do you hear?"

"Horse walking."

"Where?"

Tagee pointed eastward.

"How far?"

"Close enough that I hear."

"Dammit, how far?"

"Short ways."

Drake was about to swear again, but the sound came to him then.

"What we do now?" Tagee said.

"Close in on it."

Tagee was carrying his rifle across his saddle pommel. He said, "I see, I shoot."

"Wait first. Don't be too quick."

"I wait on you, I maybe too late."

The girl had worked frantically on the loosely tied gag that Shaw had placed in her mouth. She did it by rolling close to a jagged configuration of sharp-edged lava. She chose a protuding point near its base, inching close until she could place the side of her jaw against it. Then, desperately, she strove to catch the folded neckerchief there.

Henie whimpered with pain as the rough basalt gouged her cheek. But she did not let the hurt stop her, though it brought tears to her eyes.

Had the cloth not been tied loosely, she would never have hooked it enough to hold.

She stiffened her neck and pulled against the grasp of it

and found she was gaining slack from the loose knot. She could feel the blood running from a deep abrasion, but kept fighting for more slack until at long last, after periods of hopelessness, she worked the gag over her chin and freed her mouth.

She raised her bound wrists and tried to undo the rope with her teeth. Finally her hands were free and she went to work on her ankle bonds until she was wholly free.

They had left the horses close by, as far back as she was, to hide them from anyone approaching from over the rise.

She got unsteadily to her feet and staggered on stiff legs toward her mount.

She untethered it, and after several attempts gained the saddle.

Now, she thought, I must warn them.

To do so, she must circumvent the three men waiting in ambush. She decided to swing wide to the west of them, then to position herself on the edge of the lava bed where she could attract the attention of her brother and his partner as they appeared.

Staying concealed in the basaltic shapes, she walked her horse, trying to be as noiseless as possible.

That's when the gunfire blasted.

Tagee had aimed his weapon at sight of the rider.

Riding beside him, Drake reached out to knock the rifle upward and the shot went wild.

Tagee cursed.

Drake said, "That's your sister!"

Tagee cursed again, shocked by what he might have done.

"I maybe could have killed her!"

"Now," Drake said, "you might understand how I feel."

The girl came forward with a puzzled look.

"You fired at me?"

"It was a wild shot," Drake said. "Accidental."

Tagee appeared shaken, but he rode close and leaned over to her so they could embrace.

After a long moment they disengaged, and he said to Drake, "This my sister Henie."

Drake nodded and said to her, "My name is Drake." His eyes were on the bloodied abrasion of her cheek. "He beat you again," he said.

"No," she said. "I got cut on some lava, getting loose from being tied." She paused. "You are the man from the ghost town."

"Yes."

"The one who tried to protect me."

"And failed," he said.

"But you tried."

Tagee said, "We been ride together to get you from badmen."

"I am thankful for what you have done," she said to Drake.

"It is something I had to do," he said.

This time she was silent, giving thought to his words.

Then she said, "I remember hearing of you in Goldfield. But I did not connect that to you there in the ghost town."

For some reason he told her something now that he had not told anyone else. "I had to get away. Because of what happened."

She nodded. "I can see how that would be," she said.

Tagee spoke up then. "Sister, where are the badmen?"

"I am free," Henie said. "What is there to gain by fighting them now?"

"They must die for what they do."

The girl looked at Drake.

He chose not to say anything that would only arouse Tagee.

They had the girl, and that had been his objective.

Tagee's desire to deal out death was not shared by Drake. He lacked the desire, and more, he was still uncertain of his ability.

Seeing his apparent reluctance, the girl appealed directly to her brother.

"Please, my brother," she said in their native tongue, "do as I wish. I do not want you to chance being killed. Either of you."

Drake did not understand the words, but the meaning was apparent from her pleading tone.

Tagee frowned, then his eyes went from his sister to stare hard at Drake, and his frown became a scowl.

Drake met the stare and saw the expression of disappointment there. Disappointment mixed with contempt.

He was angered by it enough to finally speak.

"Your sister is right," he said.

Tagee was silent for a long moment.

Then he said, "All right. Because my sister wants, I let the badmen get away. We go back."

The convicts heard the fired shot.

They drew within talking distance of each other.

"What the hell!" Longo said.

"Them bounty hunters," Huff said, "they fighting each other?"

Shaw said, "That sound came from where they could be."

"Maybe they shot the squaw by mistake," Longo said.

Shaw's face showed fury. "I'll kill the bastards."

Huff said, "We was going to do that anyways."

"It had to be them, whatever reason," Longo said. "Well, Shaw?"

"Mount up," Shaw said. "We'll ride in that direction."

"Why not just stay here like we was going to?"

"Because I said we're going to ride. This changes things."

"Not for me," Longo said. He looked at Huff. "Or for Huff neither if he's got a lick of sense."

Shaw said, "Listen, I'm the one knows where to look for that spring. Unless you stay with me, you'll damn well never find it."

"You might not either."

"I've been there before. That makes my chances a hell of a lot better."

"That's right," Huff said.

"Join us," Shaw said, "or you may end up fighting them alone."

Longo did not move at once. Then he shrugged and went toward his horse.

Drake led the way westward along their backtrail, intending to exit from the lava bed near where they had entered.

They had gone only a short way when Tagee halted them.

Drake turned to look at him, and Tagee said, "Horses, again."

Drake could hear them, too.

"Maybe now they been chase us," Tagee said.

"That could be because of me," Henie said.

"What you mean?" her brother said.

"Their leader wants to keep me."

"Keep you?"

In a few words she tried to explain Shaw's change of feeling.

Both men looked shocked.

Then quick anger came into her brother's voice as he said, "You make him think it can be?"

She hesitated before saying, "Only to help me get a chance to escape."

Tagee's face was hard as he considered this.

Drake said, "We'll make a stand here where we've got some cover."

Henie said, "I hoped they wouldn't come after me."

"Well, it appears they did," Drake said.

His eyes swept their surroundings, settling on a stretch of lava that afforded some protection.

"Over there," he said.

They waited as the sounds came closer, and then suddenly the three convicts appeared.

"Let them get close," Drake said.

They were fifty yards away when Tagee could wait no longer. He fired and missed.

Drake hesitated.

Tagee exposed himself for another shot, and his arm was grazed by a bullet from one of the attackers. He fell back.

Henie saw this and yelled at Drake, "Shoot!"

But there was no need for her urging.

Without thought, as Tagee took the bullet, Drake shot Longo, who'd fired it, out of his saddle. When Longo hit the ground, he never moved.

The convicts' horses were spooked by the shooting, and Huff's shied in front of Shaw just as Drake shot again.

Huff fell as Longo had, shot between the eyes.

At that moment Shaw made a direct charge toward the rampart, firing as he came. A bullet struck Drake in the left side of his chest.

But even as it did, his own shot hit Shaw in his right arm, shattering his elbow. Shaw's weapon dropped from his hand.

Shaw turned and fled from the scene.

Drake had one final glimpse of Shaw's bloody right arm as the big convict disappeared among the lava.

Then all went black.

*   *   *

Drake recovered consciousness as Henie, with her brother's help, tried to staunch the blood flow from his critical wound. Tagee was only slightly hurt.

Packing the wound was difficult to do, since all they had were a couple of flour sacks in which Drake had been carrying food supplies from the stop at Antelope Wells.

Tagee's mind seemed to be only half on their efforts.

Even as they worked, he said, "Them two dead ones, they been convicts. If so, have reward, I think. I get their horses, we take bodies in."

"We have no time to waste. This man is seriously hurt. He could die. We must get him back to that last town."

"I be quick. While you busy with Drake."

Before she could remonstrate again, he was gone, out of sight, searching for the strayed convict mounts.

Having crudely bandaged Drake, she was slightly relieved as his bleeding lessened. She remained, sitting cross-legged beside him, stroking his forehead and holding his gun hand.

This was the hand that triggered the shots that brought to an end the agonizing ordeal she had been through. This was the man to whom she would be ever grateful.

She was suddenly aware that her brother had returned with the two horses. He brought them to where the bodies lay and was roughly hoisting the corpses across their saddles.

He lashed them there, and led them to where she was.

The mounts were spooky with their cargos, and he had trouble tethering them until he and Henie could lift Drake to seat his own mount.

Eventually they were all on horseback and set out in single file along the trail back to the Wells.

Tagee led, holding the lead rope of the convict horses which were tied together. Behind them Henie held the reins of Drake's horse as he clung with his good hand to his saddle horn.

She kept twisting to look at him, fearful he would lose consciousness and fall.

The agony of his wound showed in his face, but he held on as the miles went slowly by.

She felt a pride in his capability to do so.

She had known he had compassion; why else would he have set out alone to rescue her? And now he was showing he was tough. It was a mix of qualities that she had not often encountered among men.

By late afternoon she sensed he could no longer hang on, and she called out to her brother to halt.

Once they had taken Drake from his saddle, his weakness was apparent. They placed him in the scant shade they could find in the greasewood.

He lay unmoving, either asleep or in a coma throughout the night.

And she lay beside him, listening to his heavy breathing, afraid it would cease.

Tagee lay a few feet away. Before dark he had seen her taking her chosen place, and it had brought a frown to his face.

But he had said nothing.

In the morning they found it necessary to cut loose one of the reins by which she led Drake's horse and to use it to lash him to the cantle of his saddle.

The hours went by again, and thirst had become a constant, with the last of their water gone.

Then, abruptly, they sighted ahead the crude structures of the Wells.

Several townsmen saw them riding in, bodies draped over saddles, and a bloodstained and near-unconscious man, slumped head down and limp, tied to his saddle.

"Hell!" one said. "Them's all fellers passed through here a few days back."

"Three of them was in better shape then," another said.

"Even the Paiute's got blood on him."

It was Henie who spoke up. "Is there a doctor here?"

"Ain't none. And you got one there looks in bad shape."

"He is," she said. "And without a doctor he may die."

"We only got Whitside, runs the livery. He's done some veterinary doctoring. Pulled through a few injured miners in his time. I'll go fetch him."

"Them dead ones is sure stinking," one of the men said. "Better get them buried quick."

Tagee spoke then. "They escaped convicts. Got to be identify first."

"Identified by who?"

"Lawman some kind."

"Why?"

"May be reward."

"Ain't no lawman here, either."

Henie and Tagee, both dismounted now, were untying Drake to lift him down. A couple of the townsmen stepped forward to help.

The liveryman had seen the crowd and came hurrying toward them.

He saw Drake's condition and said, "Leave him horseback till we get him to the hotel across the way. I'll look at him there. By god, they must have had a real shoot-out!"

One of the crowd said, "Hey, there comes the stage, pulling up there too."

Tagee was leading Drake's horse as Henie and a helper clutched Drake's belt to keep him from slipping.

The stage driver was Joad; as he saw them approaching, he jumped down from his seat.

As they neared him he looked shocked and said, "Ain't that Drake?"

"That him," Tagee said.

Whitside said, "He told me he was on the trail of three hardcases. It looks like he got two of them."

Joad was close enough now to appraise Drake's physical state.

"Looks like they damn near got him."

"I'll tell you after I get him laid out and examine him," the ostler said.

Joad said, "I can take him to Goldfield on my return trip."

"I ain't sure he can stand any more rough riding. The girl says he's got a bullet lodged in him."

"Have you ever taken one out?"

"I took two out one time from a feller who got in a gun-fight."

They got Drake inside the hotel and the owner showed them to a room. Once laid out on a bed, Drake passed out from exhaustion and shock.

The ostler was a long time examining the wound.

Finally he said, "It's a toss-up. Bullet smashed a rib and appears to have been deflected. But it still reached into his chest cavity. How far, I can't tell."

"Can you do what's needed?" Henie said.

"I got to be honest," the liveryman said. "It'd be beyond my experience, by far."

Joad said, "I'll make an immediate return run to Gold-field. We've got doctors there."

Whitside was silent for a long moment. Then he said, "Believe me, I'd like to say yes to that."

"Do you?" Henie said.

Whitside shook his head. "The shape he's in, he'd never survive the trip. That's my opinion."

Joad said then, "Do you know who he is?"

"Said his name was Drake when he bought my horses."

"He's the trick shooter who accidentally killed his woman while performing in Goldfield."

Whitside looked startled. "I heard about that. But I never put the two together."

"If you can save him," Joad said, "it'd make you big in a news story."

"I ain't interested in anything like that."

Henie said, "Can you save him?"

"I'm willing to try. But even if I can, he'll need some careful nursing."

There was a silence as she weighed her competence, and then she said, "I will give him that."

CHAPTER 9

WHITSIDE WAS GONE for a few minutes, then returned with a kit of veterinary surgeon's instruments.

Joad, who had seen such before, said, "My God!"

"They'll have to do," the ostler said.

The others seemed to accept that fact, but there was great concern on the girl's face.

Noting this, Whitside said, "Miss, you can help by handing me the tools as I need them."

For her benefit, he briefly touched and named those he might need.

He said to Tagee and Joad, "You two can hold him down if or when he regains consciousness. I don't have any anesthetic."

He took up a probe from the kit. Time passed.

He called for a scalpel, which Henie handed to him; she watched with fixed gaze as he began to cut into the torn flesh.

Drake squirmed suddenly, and Whitside cursed as the two men standing by reached out to hold him steady.

More time passed as the liveryman worked in silence, sweat heavy on his face from stress.

He called for pincers and began removing pieces of rib bone and dropping them into a pan.

He began cutting again, and Drake tried to squirm, groaning sharply as Tagee and Joad struggled to hold him still.

Then, finally, Whitside asked for forceps, drew forth with them a misshapen bullet, and threw it into the pan of bone fragments.

Drake began to mumble and curse as the ostler cleaned the wound with carbolic acid.

Then it was over, and they all relaxed. All except Drake, who fell into a deep sleep.

Joad agreed to make an immediate return trip to Goldfield, with the swollen and smelly bodies of the two dead convicts wrapped in scraps of tarpaulin and shoved into the rear boot of his stage.

It was Tagee's insistence that brought him around to agreeing to do it.

"Drake and me got reward coming, I think," the Paiute said. "But got to prove it. Show to sheriff in Goldfield."

The fact that there were no passengers booked on the trip lessened any objection Joad might have had.

As they loaded the corpses, Tagee, who seemed to have acquired a hint of arrogance at having taken part in the shoot-out, said, "You go fast with stage, don't be so much stink that way."

Joad scowled at the advice, not sure if it was a joke or not.

But he made no rejoinder. After all, he did not yet know the details of what part the Indian had taken in the gunfight. He might be as much a hero as was Drake.

For three days after the surgery, as Drake remained in the hotel, the proprietor refrained from any comment concerning payment for rent or meals. Nor about Henie's constant vigil in his room.

He then broached the subject with studied casualness.

"Did Drake have any money on him, miss?"

"I thought you'd be asking," she said, trying to sound casual, too. She was well aware of hotel management policies from her work as a menial in Goldfield.

"And?"

"Almost none. A very few dollars."

"I was afraid of that."

"He mentioned this," she said, "in one lucid period when he became aware of his predicament. He spoke of a bank account in Goldfield, on which he signed a bank draft he was carrying. I gave it to Joad to submit. He'll have no money until Joad makes his next trip."

"Well," the hotel man said, "based on what we know about him as a show performer, the camp's merchants and I most likely will extend credit until then."

"We can remain here then?"

He hesitated, then said, "Missy, you are Indian, no?"

"Yes," she said.

"You know the accepted rules regarding your kind."

"I know. I have worked in hotels."

"Indians are not allowed as guests."

"I am taking care of a wounded man. Giving him the care he needs for his recovery."

"You are also sleeping in his room."

"On the floor," she said. Then, "In his condition do you think there is the possibility of immoral behavior?"

He hesitated before saying, "I have seven other guests here. They may object."

Her face hardened. "Ask them," she said.

By agreement with Whitside, Tagee had been sleeping at the livery, where their horses were stabled. He had been living on the last of the rations gleaned from their saddlebags.

Each day he looked in on Drake. And on his sister.

That he did not like her devotion to Drake was apparent from his manner. But he said nothing about it to her.

She thought she knew why: he had his mind on the possibility of sharing in a reward. Well, he deserved a part of it. He had exchanged fire with the convicts, had been wounded, if only slightly. The same bullet that grazed him could have killed him just as well.

He was in the hotel room with her when the owner came in.

He looked at Tagee and nodded, then turned to Henie.

"I have talked to the guests," he said.

She waited in silence.

"The circumstances being what they are, they seem to have no objection. I mean on account of Drake needing care."

She nodded briefly.

"However," he said, "as his condition improves, it would be best if you can find a vacant miner shack to take up residence in."

"*If* his condition improves," she said.

"You have doubt?"

"I've never been nurse to a wounded man before."

"All right," he said. "We'll leave it at that."

He left, and Tagee said, "What he mean—take up resident?"

She didn't reply.

"Damn!" he said. "I don't like thing like that."

"My brother, it will be like that until he is well."

There was a strength in her words that he recognized from past experience. He knew her mind was made up on this.

He scowled, but said, "I stay, too, then. But I got only few dollars, and I got to eat. I ask already about job as mucker in a mine. One leaser he say he hire me maybe. I go see him again now."

"That would be good," she said.

A few days passed, and surprisingly, Joad's stage returned on a special run. Two news reporters had been sent by the rival editors of the *Chronicle* and the *Sun*, Goldfield's leading papers.

Joad also brought with him a sizable amount of money, proceeds of Drake's cashed bank draft, and a Goldfield doctor. Dr. Ramsey had a drinking problem and may have had hopes of restoring his fading reputation by caring for a patient who might become a news figure.

The stage made its routine stop in front of the hotel to discharge its passengers.

The hotel owner came out to greet them.

Joad said, "Have you got accommodations for these three?"

"I've got two rooms vacant."

"Could be a problem."

Joad introduced the passengers. "This man with the satchel is Dr. Ramsey. These others are reporters from the Goldfield newspapers." He paused. "Rival papers."

"Rival papers? Will they share a room?" The hotelman addressed the two as he spoke.

"We're rivals, not enemies," Boyle from the *Chronicle* said.

"We'll share, if you make the charge accordingly," said Hargrove from the *Sun*.

"Yes, sir, gentlemen. That I will."

"We understand John Drake is quartered here," Hargrove said.

"That he is, gentlemen."

"That's what we came for."

Joad said worriedly, "I don't know what his condition is."

"He's some better," the hotel owner said.

The doctor said, "I'll be glad to check on him."

"You might have to fight the girl for that."

Joad said, "Henie is still caring for him, I take it?"

"Hardly ever leaves his side."

Once registered and assigned rooms, the new arrivals asked at the desk to see Drake.

"I'll look into it" was the reply.

Joad, meanwhile, had driven the stage to the station to release the team.

When he returned, he found the three waiting impatiently in the small lobby.

Dr. Ramsey accosted him at once.

"Might I suggest, driver, that a patient as critically wounded as I have been informed, could be in dire need of my immediate attention?"

Boyle said, "We've been told he is sleeping, and the woman caring for him will not let him be awakened."

"Just who is she?" Hargrove said.

"She's the girl he rescued from the convicts," Joad said. "It appears she is extremely grateful."

Boyle said, "I sense the possibility of a romance here."

Joad appeared struck by the thought.

"Does the idea surprise you?"

"Well, yes. It does."

"Why? A grateful woman and a heroic man—it's a natural mix, don't you think?"

"I suppose," Joad said. "Except maybe because she is a Paiute Indian."

There was a brief silence.

Then the reporter said, "It wouldn't be without precedent, you know." He paused. "Are you familiar with the story of Sarah Winnemucca, the Paiute girl who became nationally famous as an activist for her people's rights? Became a lecturer. Even went to Washington to see the Secretary of the Interior with her grievances. Met the president. She married a white army officer who befriended her."

Joad said, "I know about Sarah, of course."

"So when do we get to see her, and her patient."

"Let me go in alone and see. I've got money for Drake."

He made his way toward their room.

Henie, at the sound of his voice, immediately opened the door.

He handed her several packets of currency, then looked toward the bed.

Drake appeared to have just awakened; he turned his head to look at Joad.

He said hoarsely, "Glad to see you brought that. Thanks."

"Glad to do it, John." Joad turned back to Henie. "How's he doing?"

"Improving a little each day," she said.

"A doctor came in on the stage with me."

"A doctor?"

"He is anxious to examine your patient."

"I would welcome that," Henie said.

Joad said, "John?"

"Why not?" Drake said.

"I'll fetch him then," Joad said, and left the room.

He returned in a few minutes with Ramsey, who carried his medical case.

Joad introduced him.

Drake stirred agitatedly on the bed.

Henie noted this and said anxiously, "What's wrong?"

It was Ramsey who answered. "We have met. It was I who was called to the theatre stage when his woman was shot."

Drake said in a disturbed voice, "To pronounce her dead, Doctor!"

"Sadly, it was so," Ramsey said. "There was nothing I could do."

Drake seemed to be struggling to accept this.

Finally, he said, "I understand that. I would not imply differently."

"What happened still weighs heavily on him," Henie said. "I know from hearing his words while he was delirious."

Ramsey said, "From what the driver here has told me, a heavy-caliber bullet was removed from the cavity of his chest."

"Yes," Henie said.

"By a veterinary?"

"Liveryman," Joad corrected.

The doctor shook his head, but said, "I've known of other cases here in the West where amateur surgery has saved lives. But I am always a little astounded."

He moved toward the bed and touched the covers.

"May I, Mr. Drake?"

"Go ahead," Drake said.

Henie came to stand nearby.

Protective, Joad thought, and his mind went back to the earlier words of the *Chronicle* reporter concerning romance.

As the doctor uncovered the crude bandaging, Henie said, "We had to use whatever cloths we could gather. Flour sacks, anything."

"So I see. With your permission, I'll remove them to see the present condition of the wound. I have suitable bandaging in my bag for replacement."

He carefully undid the wrappings, exposing the mutilated flesh. He studied it for a long time.

"It is healing and there appears to be no infection. At this stage one can't expect more than that. Barring unforeseen complications, his recovery from now on will be a matter of rest. He appears to be a man of strong physique and generally good health."

He began rebandaging the wound.

"I will have to meet the veterinary and commend him on his effort."

"Liveryman," Joad said.

"Even more astounding," the doctor said.

He nodded to Henie and took a last look at Drake.

"He has fallen asleep again, I see. Best thing for him. There are two reporters wanting to see him. I'll tell them they'll have to wait a bit."

"Thank you, Doctor," Henie said.

*   *   *

The two reporters continued to wait in the lobby after Ramsey had given them the message.

They had watched as he exited into the street.

"I understand he was well regarded once, before liquor got to be too much for him," Boyle said.

The *Sun* reporter stepped to the doorway and looked out. "Heading for the saloon," he said.

"Sounded disappointed that there was no need of his services here."

"Could have been a boost back to respectability for him, had there been. My suspicion has been that's the reason he offered to make the trip down here."

"Mine too."

Again they waited. Over a period of time they each made a trip up to Drake's room. Joad had left, but Henie informed them Drake was still not to be disturbed.

Impatience was getting to them.

Boyle finally said, "I could do with a drink myself."

"We might go get a quick one," Hargrove replied.

"Wonder if Ramsey is still there?"

"I'd be willing to gamble on it."

They left the hotel and went up the street.

At a table by himself, the doctor was half slumped in his chair with a partially empty bottle in front of him.

They went to the bar and ordered a whiskey each from the barkeep, then looked over at the table.

"Want to join him?"

"Why not? Might be a story in him."

They crossed over and took chairs opposite the doctor. He looked up with drunken eyes.

"Gentlemen," he said.

"How you doing, Doc?" Boyle said.

"You boys interview the patient yet?"

"Not yet, Doc."

"Haven't got a story then, eh?"

"That's right," Hargrove said.

Ramsey poured himself a full glass and downed most of it.

"Then maybe I can give you one. About a Goldfield doctor who traveled down here and was able to give desperately needed medical attention to the heroic John Drake. Attention without which he could have relapsed fatally."

"Is that what really happened, Doc?" Boyle said.

"You want a story, don't you? And I could use one."

Hargrove said, "We might work something like that in for you, Doc."

Ramsey was silent for a long time. He poured himself another drink and tossed it off, and his slump increased.

He seemed to have trouble with his words when he next spoke.

"Appreciate anything you can concoct for me," he said.

The two reporters left shortly afterward, leaving him asleep, his head on his arms.

As they neared the hotel, Hargrove said, "When he's sober, do you think he'd appreciate us using that story if it isn't true?"

Boyle said, "No, I don't. Sober, I don't think he's that kind of a man."

CHAPTER 10

THE TWO NEWSMEN met Joad just as they reached the hotel porch.

He said, "I was just setting out to find you. Drake's ready to talk to you now."

They followed him to the room. Henie was still standing by, a fact neither of them overlooked.

"Ask your questions, gentlemen, and I'll try to answer them," Drake said. "With Henie's help. And Joad's too, because he has probably learned some more about the convicts from Sheriff Ingalls in Goldfield."

Joad said, "Only that there is a reward on them. Two thousand each had been posted, dead or alive. Be a short time at least until the money is paid. Ingalls is seeing to it with the prison officials."

Both reporters were making notes.

One of them said, "What about the one who got away?"

"Same price on his head if he's caught or killed," Joad said.

"Rumor has it he was shot also," Boyle said.

"Yes," Drake said.

"By you or the Injun?" Hargrove said, then added quickly to Henie, "Excuse me, ma'am, I meant to say your brother."

"My brother's name is Tagee," she said without rancor.

But Drake frowned and said, "We were both shooting at them."

"But who hit him?" Hargrove said. "You must understand that's important to the news story."

Henie said, "My brother missed. Mr. Drake hit all three.

82

The leader, Jack Shaw, got away with a useless right arm after wounding John."

"Was Shaw badly wounded?" Boyle said to Drake.

"I only had a glimpse, but my impression is he was."

"Then the Injun—I mean Tagee—actually hit none of them?" Hargrove said.

"We were both shooting," Drake said again.

Hargrove shrugged and added to his notes.

Boyle said, "You are neither a lawman nor a bounty hunter. The question I have is why you were pursuing the three escaped convicts?"

Drake was silent.

Henie said, "He realized I had been abducted by them, and took it upon himself to rescue me."

Boyle nodded as if this reinforced a preconception, and said to her, "Permit me to say so, miss, but I can see why. You are an attractive girl."

His compliment seemed to make no impression on her.

Joad said, "Drake was living alone in the ghost town of Tawich. The convicts came by, mistreating her in his presence."

Again Boyle nodded, adding this to his notes.

Hargrove, as if suddenly remembering he and Boyle were rivals, jotted something on his own notepad.

Then he said, "And why, Mr. Drake, were you living in Tawich?"

Joad said, "Do you have to ask that? You must recall what happened at the Hippodrome Theatre a few months back."

Hargrove did not reply, but he added another note, as did Boyle.

And so gradually the reporters mined the details of the John Drake story.

Just as they were about to leave, Tagee appeared in soiled working clothes.

He said to Henie, "I just finish shift as mucker, and hear newspaper people been here."

He looked at the reporters. "You want to ask me about things happen? You know I been hit by bullet, too?"

"We heard you were grazed by one," Hargrove said.

"Graze? Yeah, but little bit other way I been dead. You write about, huh?"

"Sure," Boyle said. "We'll include what you did in our stories."

Tagee turned suddenly to Joad. "What did you find out about reward, huh?"

"Two thousand for each dead one."

"I get half?" Tagee said to Drake.

"Yes," Drake said.

Tagee nodded his satisfaction, then said, "When?"

Joad said, "The prison warden will be seeing to it."

"Will be?"

"Is."

"How long he take?"

"I don't know. Short while, I was told," Joad said.

Tagee's satisfied look had disappeared.

Drake was watching him, and said, "I can loan you money to live on."

"But what about my sister?"

"I will take care of her."

"For why?"

"For the care she is giving me."

"And then?"

"We will see," Drake said.

"*We will see* is part I don't like."

Henie said, "Brother, you are insolent."

"What that means?"

"It means, my brother, for you to be quiet. Please?"

Boyle was again scribbling at his notes.

Hargrove said to Tagee, "Drake made a success of your effort to rescue your sister. Do you not feel an amount of gratitude for that?"

"Sure I do."

"You don't sound like you credit him enough."

"I credit him plenty," Tagee said. "But I want credit for what I do, too."

"For the reward, right?"

"It too."

"By god," Hargrove said, "you are frank enough about it!"

"I got mine claim I work. Need money to live while I do."

"I see."

Little by little the newsmen drew forth the details of the mission the two had accomplished.

By that time Drake was showing exhaustion.

Henie had been watching him closely and immediately spoke up.

"That's enough for now. Later, perhaps. Or better yet, tomorrow, if you wish."

The reporters and Joad left.

Tagee remained.

"You too, brother," Henie said.

He seemed about to object, but then made his way to the door and exited without comment.

When she looked at Drake, he had once more faller asleep.

The reporters ended up in the lobby.

Hargrove said, "Did you get all you needed?"

"Almost."

"What else is there to know?"

Boyle said, "I would like to know what happened to Shaw after he left their sight."

Shaw's agony was excruciating. It drove him into shock, and it was only when he fell forward over the saddle horn that he became conscious of his surroundings.

He was aware of the familiarity of the lava-strewn terrain. Through his dim consciousness slowly filtered its significance.

There was green foliage here, and that meant one thing.

The spring, he thought. The one he had hoped to find, and there it was.

He sat on his horse, staring down, as his mount nuzzled in a small basaltic pool of water.

He needed water himself. He needed to fill his canteen.

But the agony of his arm hung as an obstacle to his dismounting.

The horse continued to drink, and somewhere in his mind was the thought it might founder itself if not briefly detained.

He pulled on the rein with his good left hand, but the horse fought the bit until he increased the tug. It threw up its head rebelliously.

He got it a few feet away from the pool, but he had to hold it there, reins tight, weighing his ability to make a quick dismount with a dangling, useless, agony ridden arm.

He stayed fixed by indecision until even the horse became impatient and tried to twist its neck.

He swore then, and in a fit of self-fury, he drew his right foot from the stirrup and twisted to haul his leg over the haunch, striking the helpless arm as he did so and crying out.

But he made it to the ground still clutching the reins. He moved to the side of the pool, and somehow lowered himself prone enough so that he and the horse were sucking up water side by side.

He lay there awhile before some instinct for survival caused him to move. He had to go on, to get to where he might find treatment for his arm.

He knew that without help he would die.

Knowing that, and telling himself that he was tough Jack Shaw, he forced himself to somehow fill his canteen and after several failures to remount his saddle.

He was once more on the faint trace he believed he had years earlier traveled. By god!—he would get where he had started for, or die trying.

He was not going to let a bullet fired by that goddamn spook from the ghost town stop him.

It wasn't a bounty hunter or two who had been tracking him.

At the moment of the exchange of fire, he had recognized the face behind the gun that shot him.

Who the hell was he? And why had he persisted in his pursuit? Only because Shaw had pistol-whipped him? Hell, he had spared killing him because he reminded Shaw of somebody else who once did him a favor.

That had been a mistake. Maybe the worst one of a life of many.

If they ever met again, Shaw thought, he'd even the score.

As dusk came, he managed to dismount again and tether the horse to some creosote, struggling one-handed to tie the reins.

He made no attempt to unbridle it, and collapsed at once a few feet away.

The night was full of delirious dreams that came and went, and the morning was scarcely better. He went through the evening's motions in reverse, each movement accomplished as if he were drunk. Untying the tethering reins almost defeated him, but it drove him into enough anger to clamber wildly onto his shying horse.

Once there, all the fire went out of him as he let the animal pick the trail.

How far did he have yet to go?

He tried to guess, but his memory was unclear. Thirty miles? God, he hoped not. Twenty?

He was able to reach his canteen a few times and uncork it with his teeth, but the last time he found it empty.

He had not been able to give any to the horse, and now he feared the animal might fail him.

As might he himself. He felt engulfed by a weakness that forbade his trying to dismount again, for any reason. He was certain that once off the horse, he'd never have the strength to remount.

He had lost much blood in the beginning. Soaked into his sleeve, it had dried stiff.

But now the bleeding seemed to have stopped. That brought him a moment of panic. Hadn't he once heard that loss of blood supply to a wound would cause the onslaught of gangrene?

He wished he could remember for sure.

The blazing sun had crossed most of the sky when, in a brief spell of lucidity, he saw the trees.

He didn't believe them, but he could see them.

He kept moving toward them, not through effort of his own, but by will of the horse he was riding. He had been out of his head for untold miles, he guessed.

Riding in oblivion, remaining seated on horseback by some subconscious directive, he had arrived at a stand of cottonwood trees. At first he wasn't sure whether they were real or imagined.

Then came the sense that this was a familiar location. He was certain there was a spring ahead! Not just any springs, he thought then. His springs. The springs of his destination.

Indian Springs, the warm-springs oasis. Where he had once stayed at the small hotel run by a retired outlaw acquaintance.

The thought brought him to full awareness.

Would the old acquaintance still be here? Would he still be alive?

Shaw guided the horse to the hitch rack in front of the hotel.

He sat there then, debating whether to attempt to dismount.

The hotel verandah was empty, and after a while he made the try, got himself on the near side, but with his left boot still caught in its stirrup. He clung there, unable to disengage it.

A man came out on the porch and stared at him.

He called, "Can't you make up your mind?"

Shaw stared back at him, giving no answer.

The man on the porch was studying the dangling, blood-soaked sleeve. He said then, "Hold on, fellah," stepped down, and moved toward him.

He reached for the stirrup and freed it from Shaw's boot.

Shaw looked at him and saw an old man, old but still with a leanness some one-time riders kept.

Shaw said, "Buck Lemon still run this place?"

"Yeah, he does. You know him?"

"Used to," Shaw said. "We rode together once."

"Been five-six-seven years, Jack."

"All of that, Buck."

"Let's get you inside off the street and hid out in a room. Word is, even here, that you busted out of the pen."

"Kind of afraid of that. Was hoping to reach Arizona before it spread."

"That arm of yours is beginning to stink," Buck said, helping him onto the verandah and into the hotel. "It ain't a good sign."

"You got a doctor around here?"

"We got Doc Brent. You remember him? He's went straight after doing a term in Yuma Territorial. He's got an office in his shack down the street."

"I don't know as I'd trust somebody that's went straight."

"Fellah, you don't have much choice by the smell of that arm."

Shaw was silent.

"Besides," Buck Lemon said, "Doc ain't gone *that* straight."

"Good to hear," Shaw said. His voice was weak.

"God!" Lemon said. "I better get hold of Brent pretty quick!"

*   *   *

Doc Brent was a small wiry man of middle age.

His hair was gray, as was his neatly clipped mustache.

He wore metal-rimmed glasses and a dark suit; he had based much of his career on treating bullet wounds among the outlaw fraternity and keeping his mouth shut about it.

He had actually attended an Eastern medical school before coming West. He had gained experience first with mining casualties in Arizona, although occasionally confronted with gunshot wounds, with which he seemed more adept than most of his lesser-trained frontier peers.

In time he found himself increasingly sought out by crime participants, whose adventurous exploits seemed to fascinate him. So much so, that he sometimes allowed himself to be recruited by holdup gangs to accompany them, for a share of the loot, in case of urgent need.

It was exciting and, briefly, profitable. Until, after one train robbery attempt that failed, he was accosted by lawmen as he was treating three of the perpetrators.

He was brought to trial on an accessory-after-the-fact charge, convicted, and sent to the Arizona prison.

He always thought he'd been railroaded by an overzealous prosecution, but after doing a three-year sentence he had given up any active participation in outlawry and moved to Nevada.

But he had been left with a feeling about the law that kept him sympathetic toward those who flaunted it.

Doc Brent, brought to the hotel by Lemon, stood beside him looking down on the figure on the hotel bed.

He said, "Yes, I remember meeting him once. A long time back. We've got to get him down to my office."

"How?" Lemon said. "I got guests here. They see him being carried down there, they'll be curious."

"I'll have to get my buggy hitched," Doc Brent said. "When I come back, we'll have to move fast, try to get him out without being seen. If we are, you'll have to make some excuse about him being a stranger had an accident. Not everybody knows about him breaking out, I hope."

"Probably so. Wouldn't expect him to show up here, anyway. Most of them busted out been found over Owens Valley way, in California."

The guest list was small, and the transfer of Shaw was done with no apparent witnesses.

"What's to be done, Doc?" Lemon said when Shaw was laid out on an operating table.

He was now in a coma.

"Stand by," Brent said. "If I find what I think I'm going to, I'll need your help."

"Gangrene, ain't it?"

"If so," Doc said, "the arm will have to come off."

CHAPTER 11

THE TWO REPORTERS and the doctor returned to Goldfield on Joad's stage.

Once there, the doctor dropped from view, but Boyle and Hargrove each filed a story.

Hargrove's appeared in the *Sun*, and except for the wording, differed little from what Boyle wrote in the *Chronicle*.

The *Chronicle* piece read in part:

TRAGIC TRICK SHOT IS HERO IN RESCUE OF GIRL!

John Drake, the professional trick shot, who recently lost his bride-to-be in a fatal miss on the Hippodrome stage, has killed two of the Carson prison escapees after an arduous track-down in the Ralston Desert.

In the fierce shoot-out a third convict escaped, critically wounded, after wounding Drake.

Drake is recovering now in Antelope Wells, in the care of a young Paiute woman whom he rescued from captivity by the desperados.

In Hargrove's piece the caption read:

TRAGIC TRICK SHOT IS HERO IN KILLING OF ESCAPED CONVICTS!

John Drake, the professional trick shot who a few weeks ago had a misfire during a theatre performance, which cost the life of his fiancée, is back in the news, having killed two escaped convicts from the Nevada State Prison and wounded seriously a third who got away.

Drake, it appears, had some help from a Paiute man who

was on the same trail because the convicts had abducted
his sister.

In a matter of days the story had been picked up by newspapers in several towns throughout Nevada.

Goldfield personages were soon besieged by telegraph
inquiries from outside the state. A national wire service
took it on and made John Drake a celebrity.

At first the story stressed his encounter with the convicts,
with only shadowy mention of the tragedy on the Hippodrome stage. But this quickly became a tantalizing part of
the whole.

The oblivion Drake had sought in the ghost town was
taken from him. The memory of Molly's death was once
again always with him.

He and Henie had left the hotel—his savings were not
unlimited, and when a vacant miner hut was available they
moved into it.

By now he was up and around, and there was some hesitation on his part about the propriety of her continuing to
live with him. But she had to have a place to stay and
showed no hesitancy herself.

The people of the small town seemed to accept this,
partly because the pair had shared a hotel room during his
recovery and partly because of his having rescued her
from the convicts. There were few women in Antelope
Wells, and most of them, as did the men, appeared to feel
Drake was only receiving just due for his deed. Some of
them might even have been envious.

But these conjectures were incorrect.

Drake and Henie, though under one roof, were still
sleeping apart.

Each was grateful for what the other had done. He for
the aid she had given to his recovery, she for his rescue
of her.

This mutual gratitude went unspoken between them. It
was something so strong that there was no need for words.

Sometimes her eyes lingered on him as she sensed his returning vitality. She would have a brief arousal, only to lose it abruptly in the nightmare memory of being brutally raped by the three convicts.

And when he, in turn, treated her kindly but made no overture, she understood, knowing the crushing blow he suffered by the loss of the woman he loved, dead by his own hand.

Tagee voiced an objection to their arrangement, but it had no effect on his sister, and he more or less tolerated it sullenly.

He continued to work in the mines, although he questioned Drake about when they might expect the reward money.

"I got gold claim, my own," he said. "Want work it."

"I understand," Drake said.

"You understand don't want be mucker rest my life?"

"Yes," Drake said.

"Reward one chance I got future, goddammit!"

Tagee's words started Drake wondering about his own future for the first time since that fatal shot in Goldfield. Without Molly he had not wanted a future. Now he knew he had to go on. But doing what?

He had worked at various occupations during his twenties until he realized his talent for target shooting; he'd developed it with devoted practice to make himself a paid performer for these past five years.

Son of a hardware merchant in Kansas, he had left home at eighteen, making his way west to Winnemucca, Nevada, where he spent two years learning to buckaroo on a ranch.

He'd clerked in a local hardware store after a seasonal layoff. Then he became briefly a bank teller, before returning to Kansas to run the family hardware business upon the sudden death of his father. It was a business that provided him with a wholesale price on gun ammunition, great quantities of which were required to perfect a would-be trick shot's skills.

He first performed professionally with a small-time touring Wild West show that passed through his town, one of several two-bit imitators of Buffalo Bill's successful enterprise.

When the show folded in bankruptcy several towns later, he landed a spot in a vaudeville show house, and that began his career on theatre circuits, which eventually brought him back to Nevada, and to Goldfield.

One thing was certain: he would not return to being a trick-shot artist. The remembrance of what had happened at the Hippodrome still weighed too heavily on him for that.

In the few weeks he had been recovering there had been a change in the pace of mine activity in the town. It all began with prospectors who searched out possible ore-bearing ledges, filed claims, and did a bit of preliminary digging as they subsisted on a grubstake.

If ore was found, and its worth showed the possibility of profit, word went out to potential speculative leasers.

Few original prospectors had the patience, know-how, or money to operate or develop their claims.

This is where the leasers came in, arranging to lease for a given period to work the claim with hired miners, paying the claim owners twenty to twenty-five percent of the take if the ore assayed worthwhile.

The claim owner thus ended up at the end of the lease date with a partly developed mine instead of just a surface claim.

That was the way many new mines got started.

Needless to say, the leasers sought to work fast to uncover as much high-grade ore, if any, as they could in their given time.

This led to a quick demand for manpower to dig, a demand filled within days by recurringly unemployed miners from other booms that had fizzled.

And with the miners came the unruly fringe that lived off them: drunk rollers, crooked gamblers, whores, and others.

A boomtown could be created in a matter of days. And its beginning could sometimes be its roughest.

It could be a period when the earlier residents felt overwhelmed and in need of some protection from the threat of lawlessness.

It was Whitside who came to the shack shared by Drake and Henie, and stated the problem. He brought with him the hotel owner, a mercantile proprietor, and the barkeep.

"Our population has doubled this past week," he said. "Some are honest miners, and some are the predators who followed them."

"I've noticed," Drake said.

"We want to keep things under control," Whitside said. "We've decided to chip in and hire us a constable."

"Sounds like a good idea," Drake said.

There was a short silence.

Whitside said then, "You."

"Me? I've had no law-keeping experience."

"You won't need any. Your name is now known all over the country for the way you took those convicts. It ain't likely anybody will give you much trouble."

"Much? I don't want *any*."

"It's us," the livery man said, "who'll have the trouble if there's nowhere we can turn to keep the rough element in line."

"I repeat," Drake said, "I am far from being a lawman."

"Your new reputation alone should do the job."

Drake was thoughtful. This was something he had never tried. He had been questioning himself about his future: could this be an answer? And it was Whitside, the man who had most likely saved his life, who was pleading. Could he refuse him?

With some reluctance he finally said, "I'll give it a try."

Henie, who had listened to the conversation, made no comment. When he searched her face for an indication of her feeling, he found none there. Perhaps, he thought, she shared his own uncertainty at his decision.

There was no way he could ask her in front of the townsmen—he had recovered a measure of his former pride and it prevented that. Had he recovered it sufficiently to handle the job he was being asked to do?

There was no way to know until he tried to do the job.

It was the liveryman who fashioned him a badge out of a discarded piece of shiny metal trim that had once adorned an old Mexican saddle.

Whitside had been largely correct in assuming the publicity given Drake would have its effect on his keeping the peace in Antelope Wells.

Most of the newcomers had heard of his showdown with the prison escapees. And those who hadn't were soon informed.

"Shot the living hell out of them" was the way more than one described it.

Pointing him out and identifying him by name was all that was required to gain the immediate respect of the law-abiding, and a sullen wariness from the others.

He sensed the smoldering threat of the latter and guessed they were not entirely convinced of his capability as a lawman.

They would be testing him, he was sure.

How soon and how hard, that was the question.

Whitside had made space in his small livery office for a table to be used as Drake's desk, and painted a sign to post outside that read: *John Drake, Constable.*

"What do we use for a jail?" Drake had asked.

"We'll clear out a tack room," the ostler said. "I'll get some bars put over the window, and beef up the door."

From the beginning Drake had decided that if he were to be an effective constable, he should be seen publicly and often by the people of Antelope Wells. Therefore, he set up a routine of frequent foot patrols of the town itself and occasional visits on horseback into the nearby mining area. This not only made the residents aware of his presence, but the physical exercise hastened his healing process.

He went armed with his .45 Colt and was surprised at how often the eyes of those who saw him on the street shifted from his face to the gun hanging at his side. It was as if the gun itself shared his reputation. Everyone was aware of his prior work as a trick-shot performer.

He believed this could be an asset. If they feared the weapon, they would be less likely to provoke him into using it. The townsfolk had no way of knowing that even the possibility of using his gun instilled dread in Drake.

Several days went by without incident.

And then Joad's stage arrived, bearing seven passengers. The stage service was now on an every-other-day schedule, staying overnight before returning to Goldfield.

This time one of the passengers seemed vaguely familiar to Drake, although he couldn't place him. He was dressed in a business suit, and Drake guessed him to be either a would-be merchant, a speculator, or possibly a prospective leaser. He was a clean-shaven man, perhaps Drake's age, and he did not appear to be one of the rough element. Except for the hint of familiarity in his looks, there was nothing else to single him out from the rest of the passengers.

The stage had unloaded in front of the hotel, whose keeper had long since run out of existing rooms to handle the boomtown onslaught of newcomers. To meet this growing need, he had ordered tents brought in from Beatty, and erected them behind the hotel proper.

Other new entrepreneurs had followed suit at other areas around the town.

The well-dressed stranger strode into the hotel lobby, ahead of the rest. At the registration desk, he managed to get a room vacated a few hours earlier.

Drake, who had nodded to the arrivals and followed them in, noted that the man took the room readily, even though its rate was higher than that for tent accommodations.

As the stranger looked up from writing his signature, he caught Drake's eyes on him, and met his stare. For a long moment their stares held, neither showing anything to the other.

The stranger finally turned away but did not drop his eyes before he did so. He then left as the clerk directed him to his room.

The other passengers signed in and were given the numbers of their tent spaces. As they left, Drake stepped to the desk and scanned the register, picking out the first of the new names with particular interest.

E. A. Raworth, he read.

The name meant nothing to him.

He continued his day with sporadic patrols, coming upon an active incident just as he was passing one of the new crude saloons in a rough section of town.

From within came a blast of revolver fire.

The sound had a double effect on him: He knew he had to investigate, but he dreaded doing so. This was what he'd been afraid would happen in such a case, and he forced himself toward the structure's open doorway.

Inside were only two customers, two freighters whom he had seen unloading cargo from their respective wagons earlier that day.

They lay now on the dirt floor, unmoving, a few feet apart, in front of the improvised bar of planks laid across barrel tops.

There appeared to be no blood on either stretched-out body.

But close beside each a handgun was lying.

Drake eyed the scene and spoke to the heavyset barkeep, who still held a long, heavy club in his hand.

"They shoot each other?"

"No," the barkeep said. "They only tried and missed."

"At six feet apart?" Drake said.

"Reckon they ain't good shots like you, Constable. I hit them both with this club before they could miss again. I was afraid they might accidentally hit someone if they kept trying long enough."

The men on the floor began to stir.

Drake bent quickly to pick up the dropped weapons.

"Were they drunk?"

"Getting that way. Seemed to be friends at first, then got to arguing what brand of chewing tobacco was best."

"Poor thing to die for," Drake said, anger in his voice.

"Ain't everything?" the barkeep said. "You going to throw them in that jerry-built jail I hear you got?"

"Till they're sober," Drake said. "I still can't see how they missed."

The barkeep gave him a long studying look, then said, "Well, Constable, missing can happen to better shots than they are, what I hear."

His sarcasm stung Drake.

He had herded the whiskey-sick freighters to the improvised holding cell at the livery.

He then sat in his part of the office, his mind on the barkeep's remark. Thinking of the Hippodrome tragedy led to memories of Molly, including how they first met.

Back then he had been doing his act with a male assistant. The man had quit and left him in need of a replacement for scheduled bookings. Drake had advertised in a local newspaper for someone, offering an opportunity to enter show business. A dozen men had applied, but all had lost interest when they found their role would mostly be that of a human target.

Just as his approaching performance dates were making him desperate, Molly had appeared.

She was an eager, attractive young woman, tired of her job as an office worker.

He had sensed she was of an adventurous nature and seemed unafraid of the risks involved.

She had been making her own way since her late teens, when both her parents had died of pneumonia. She had been an only child, with no close relatives except one male cousin from whom she maintained her distance.

At this point Drake was suddenly struck by another recollection.

There had been an occasion during that time when Molly had received a letter that disturbed her, which she had mentioned to Drake. It was from the cousin, who had learned somehow that she was about to appear in shooting performances. He had warned her of the dangers of doing so.

Drake had asked her if she wished to withdraw from the act.

She had said, "No, John. I'm not disturbed by his warning, but by his getting in touch with me again."

"What do you mean?"

"It has been a long time since I've heard from him. I made it plain to him in the past that I didn't want him to have any contact with me."

"Your own cousin?"

She was silent for a long time, then said, "That was just

it, John. He was a cousin with whom I was close when we were very young. We played together as children. But as we grew older his fondness toward me changed."

"You had a falling out?" he said.

"On my part."

"Why?"

"Because his fondness grew beyond what a cousin's feelings should be," she said. "Whenever we met and embraced it had become much more than that. I warned him this was wrong. And when he persisted in his lustful attitude, I was revolted by it.

"He still pressed his attentions, and I avoided seeing him as much as I could."

"Is he still persistent?"

"He is no longer nearby. He's now a lawman in a small town in New Mexico. He was always adept with weapons and has worn a badge in several places. But I've heard rumors he has sometimes been on the other side of the law."

Drake had remarked that it seemed the cousin still had a crush on her.

And she had replied, "That is what bothers me."

But no more was heard from the errant relative, and Molly never mentioned him again.

And until this day, Drake had forgotten him. Could not even recall his name.

Suddenly he realized why the stranger looked familiar. Something in his facial features was faintly reminiscent of Molly.

He got up from his desk and walked out the door toward the hotel.

At the registration counter, he asked if an E. A. Raworth was in.

The clerk said, "No, sir, he isn't."

"I'll try later," Drake said.

"Don't try here, sir. He checked out right after he checked in. He came back to the desk as soon as you had left, and asked your name. 'That of the man with the badge,' was the way he put it."

"You gave it to him, I presume?"

"Yes, sir. And right away he demanded his room deposit back. No argument there—he had the appearance of a man you don't trifle with. Took up his suitcase and carried it down the street after I told him there was other lodging down that way."

Drake left the hotel and walked toward the part of the town that the clerk had indicated.

It was getting dusk, and kerosene lanterns were lighted among the scattered shacks and tents.

Drake decided to stop first at the saloon where the pair of inebriated freighters had caused trouble earlier. There were a half-dozen drinkers bellied up to the planks.

The barkeep saw him enter and watched his approach, frowning.

Drake edged into a space at the near end of the bar, and the barkeep moved down to face him.

"You get them damn drunks put to bed?" he said.

"Yeah. But that clubbing you gave them could have killed them."

"If I hadn't done it, they'd have killed each other. . . . You come back to ask more questions about it?"

"No. I'm looking for a fellow who rode in on the stage today. Might have been carrying a suitcase. May have inquired about lodging."

"I ain't an information service on my customers," the barkeep said. His eyes shifted to the patron standing nearest to Drake. The barkeep could tell the patron was listening, and he was bothered by it.

"Just wanted to talk to him," Drake said. "This one was wearing a suit, looked like a businessman of some kind."

Finally the barkeep said, "Was one like that stopped in here. I told him if he was wanting a place to stay, to head down the street farther and he'd see a sign or two that might have a vacancy. He had a couple of drinks and went on his way."

"Thanks," Drake said, and turned to leave.

He took a couple of steps before the barkeep said, "Wait!"

Drake turned back.

"He came in again after you was here. After you took them two drunks to the pokey."

"He say he'd found lodging?"

"I guess he had, though he didn't say where. But he wasn't carrying his suitcase anymore."

The drinker next to Drake was still listening, and now he spoke. His words were a little slurred.

"Feller wasn't packing no suitcase then," he said. He looked at the barkeep. "He the feller was standing where the constable is standing now? Come in after I did?"

The barkeep nodded.

"No suitcase," the patron said. "This time he was packing a six-gun belted around his hips. His suit coat was open like he wanted it to be seen."

Drake looked at the barkeep. "That right?"

"Yeah. I was going to warn you, Constable, but this man interrupted. He had a few drinks this time, didn't say much. Then he asked if there was a lawman around, and if there was, did he patrol the town in the evening."

The patron said, "The barkeep here, he told him yeah."

"You got a big mouth," the barkeep said. "You know that?"

"The better to drink with," the patron said.

Drake left the saloon and walked down the now-darkened street.

The light from the lamps and lanterns within the tents and shacks gave only faint illumination for part of the way. There were stretches of darkness that were almost black.

He began to wonder if he should continue, and then it was too late.

He sensed he was being followed and turned to look back, but he could make out no figure in the shadows.

He kept walking until he entered a stretch void of any light, then stepped off the street and felt his way into a narrow walkway between two unlighted board structures.

He drew his gun.

And now a darker splotch seemed to appear in the blackness opposite the narrow recess in which he stood. He spoke out then, calling the name of the man he believed was following him.

"Raworth!"

The splotch froze, unmoving.

There was a short silence, and a voice said, "You're John Drake, ain't you?"

"I am."

"You don't remember my real name?"

"Who are you?"

"Molly's cousin."

"Why are you here?"

"She was the woman I loved."

"I remember now."

"I warned her against you."

"I remember that too."

"I been reading in the papers what you did to her in Goldfield. Do you know what it is to lose a woman you love?"

"I know."

"You killed her, you son of a bitch!"

Drake dropped to a prone position just as the gun blasted from the street.

He fired at the flash and heard the man grunt as the bullet struck him body high. He made no sound or movement again.

For a long time neither did Drake.

CHAPTER 12

KILLING THIS MYSTERY figure, E. A. Raworth, who for some unknown reason had tried to gun down the constable, added to John Drake's reputation.

Drake, determined to avoid mention of the somewhat scandalous details of Raworth's relationship to Molly, innocent though she was, had only stated to the curious that he had never met his attacker previously.

The barkeep who had spoken to the assailant revealed the latter had asked about the town lawman, even questioning if he patrolled the streets after dark. He was backed up in this statement by the bar patron, who swore he'd heard the conversation.

The general consensus was that the gunman was simply one of those psychopaths with a compulsion to achieve notoriety as a gunfighter.

That he had failed in this simply added to the fame of Drake.

And brought another visitor to Antelope Wells to see Drake.

He was sitting in his improvised office when the man entered. Drake looked up to see a well-kept, middle-aged figure in an expensive suit. Beneath his hat brim, gray hair was combed back at the temples.

"I assume you are John Drake?" he said.

"Yes."

"I am Major Bonner. Major Conrad Bonner."

Drake stood up to shake his extended hand, saying, "Army officer?"

"Retired," the major said.

"What can I do for you, Major?"

"I represent a Wild West show now touring the country." Drake was silent.

Bonner said, "*Winston's Wild West.* You perhaps have heard of us?"

"Possibly," Drake said. "Buffalo Bill Cody has had a lot of imitators."

"True," the major said. "But we of *Winston's* feel we are far above the usual run. We would consider ourselves to be a competitor rather than a mere imitator."

"Tough competition," Drake said.

"That is also true. But Cody and the rest have almost totally catered to the Eastern populace, and the Middle West. For that reason we've decided to try a tour of the West itself. Most areas have been pretty well tamed of its former wildness, but we believe people who live in the West are nostalgic about how it was."

"An interesting perspective," Drake said. "But why are you telling this to me?"

Bonner smiled. "You have received a vast amount of publicity during recent weeks. Mr. Winston, an experienced showman, knows the value this could have when it comes to drawing audiences."

"I've given up my career as a trick-shot performer, Major," Drake said. "I wouldn't be interested in any proposal you might make."

"We are prepared to make it worth your while financially," Bonner said. "Surely you don't intend to continue risking your life as a mere constable in a mining camp?"

"You spoke of the news stories," Drake said. "Do you know what happened during my last performance?"

"In Goldfield, wasn't it? Yes, we know about that. An accident that could happen to anyone, anywhere."

"Anyone? Anywhere? No, it could only happen from a misfired bullet that missed its intended target."

"Still, it was an accident," Bonner said. "Let me put it to

you bluntly. The only way you will ever rid yourself of the false guilt that haunts you is to stop trying to run from it. Come to grips with it and destroy it."

"How?"

"I'm offering you a way. Resume your career. At least try it and see what happens."

"Not interested," Drake said.

"I won't insist on your decision immediately. Our tour plans aren't finalized as yet. Tentatively, they would include California, Oregon, and Nevada."

Drake took refuge in silence again.

"Please think about it," Bonner said. "I'll be here in town for a day or two. I'll contact you again."

"My answer will be the same," Drake said.

Bonner studied him for a long moment. He had dealt with performers for several years and believed he knew what deep down made them tick.

He said, "I've been authorized to offer you star billing, and to pay you as the featured act in our show.

"You have proved yourself able to overcome tragedy, and that will add to the acclaim that will sell tickets. And every time you perform, that acclaim will grow. You can become the greatest."

This time Bonner could see in Drake's face that he had caught at his ego.

But Drake said then, "Who would be fool enough to be my target holder?"

"We will find one for you," the major said.

Bonner watched from the hotel lobby window as Constable Drake left his office next morning and set out walking his routine patrol.

He had learned the location of Drake's residence, and as he disappeared from view, Bonner headed toward it.

He reached the rented shack, eyed it critically for a moment, then approached and knocked on the door.

He had learned of the living arrangement between

Drake and the Paiute girl, which was how he thought of her. He had been thinking of her since late the previous evening, after his last words with Drake.

When she opened the door and stood before him, he was a bit struck by her attractiveness. So much the better for what he had in mind, he thought.

He gave her a warm smile, hesitating over how to address her.

She waited, sensing his confusion, and guessing his identity by the description Drake had given her last night.

"I am Major Bonner," he said finally. "I am with *Winston's Wild West*. Perhaps Mr. Drake mentioned me to you after the conversation I had with him yesterday."

"He isn't in right now, Major Bonner."

"May I ask if he spoke to you about our discussion?"

"A word or two, yes."

He studied her face, but it told him nothing.

"Tell me, ma'am, are you at ease with his being a lawman?"

"It is his choice," she said.

"This last shooting, his being attacked without a sane reason by a stranger whom he did not even know—doesn't that cause you to worry?"

"I worry, of course."

"As his woman, of course you do." He smiled. "He rescued you and you nursed him back to health. It's a very romantic story."

She appeared thoughtful, then said, sounding surprised, "A romantic story? I never thought of it as such."

"Oh, I think it is," Bonner said, "and so will everyone else who hears of it." He paused, waiting for her curiosity to grow.

And when it did, she asked as Drake had earlier, "But why are you telling this to me?"

And he gave her the same answer: "Because of the value it could have in drawing an audience."

"An audience?"

"To see John Drake, the legendary hero, thrill them with his shooting skills."

She said, "But he will not perform again."

"I am here to change his mind."

"I don't think you can."

"Maybe not," Bonner said. "But I think I could with your help."

She said, with some anger, "I would not try to influence him."

He considered this and said, "What future does he have wearing a star at fifty dollars a month? Daily risking his life for it?"

"It's what he wants," she said.

"Do you really believe that? Or is it just that he has taken the job out of necessity."

"It's his decision."

He said abruptly then, "Let me ask you this—If he would agree, would you take part in his performance?"

She looked shocked. "You mean—?"

He watched her closely as he said, "Yes. You could be the target girl."

That evening Henie told Drake that Bonner had called on her.

"To try to get my support in convincing you to join the show he represents," she said.

He looked at her closely. "And did he?"

"I told him it was your decision to make."

"Good. What else did he say?"

"Pretty much what he had said to you."

"Were you impressed?"

She was briefly silent. Then she said, "One thing stays with me, John. He referred to me as *your woman*."

A moment passed before he said, "Well?"

"Am I?"

"Aren't you?"

"Have we ever showed each other that I am?"

He thought about what she was saying. "There are things that have held me back."

"Yes, I know."

There was another pause, then he said, "It might be time to overcome that."

She reached out and touched him.

"Let's try," she said.

He took her in his arms then.

And the hungry press of her body told him what to do.

Bonner waited on the hotel porch the next morning until he saw Drake eventually go to his office, then he made his way down the street.

When Bonner entered the office, Drake was facing the door.

"You don't give a man much time, if you expect a change of decision," he said.

"I have a reason for that."

"Oh?"

"I said we'd find a willing assistant for your act."

"What, here in the Wells?"

"It so happens."

"Who?"

"Your woman."

"Henie?"

Bonner was silent until Drake said again, "Henie? You must be crazy!"

"I've talked to her. She owes you her life. It would be a way for her to repay you."

"She said that? Did you put that idea in her head?"

"I did not speak of repayment. I merely spoke of the great opportunity *Winston's* is offering you. To get back the life you appear to have abandoned."

"Did you lead her to think this was my idea?"

"Believe me, I did not. I presented it as my own, then inquired as to her feelings about it."

"My God! How could you ask her after what happened in Goldfield!"

"It's obvious she has confidence in your ability."

Drake did not speak at once. Then he said, "Well I do not. Do you understand that?"

"What *Winston's* is proposing will give you the way to regain it."

"Are you trying to say this is your motive in making your offer?"

"Of course not. Our motive is to capitalize on what we believe to be your recently increased audience appeal. And to do that, I am trying to overcome your reluctance to be a part of it."

Drake said, "I will tell you this, Major. Convincing Henie to be my assistant—"

"She convinced herself," Bonner said.

"—does your case no good."

The major shrugged. "We can get someone else as your assistant, John. But the romantic circumstances that have evolved from your recent adventures would provide a tantalizing element we could use to great effect. One we'd hate to lose."

"You think of everything, don't you?" Drake said.

"My job. And you grasp what we're after, of course. You know show business yourself."

Drake was silent.

"Your woman is intelligent. And I would appraise her as also ambitious. She quickly showed an interest in what I'm proposing. Not for herself, but for you. All women want their men to succeed." Bonner paused. "She's looking to your future, John. Yours, and hers too."

At that moment a figure appeared in the office doorway.

Tagee stood there, staring at Drake, his face set hard.

Bonner turned and gave him a curious glance.

Drake said, "What is it, Tagee?"

"I just been talk with my sister. What you try to do with her?"

"What did she tell you?"

"She say she going be in shooting act with you."

"We were discussing it, yes."

"You better discuss it *no!* You hear?"

Bonner said, "I presume this is the brother of your woman, John?" He gave Tagee a friendly smile as the latter faced him, and went on, "The man who took a courageous part in the shootout against the convicts. Suffered a wound himself, I understand. A hero in his own right."

He extended his hand.

Tagee did not take it. Instead, he said, "You full of bull, hey?"

The major's smile faded.

"You been the one make trouble?" Tagee said. "You been the one put damn-fool idea in her head?"

The major struggled down a flare of temper and said, "It was a suggestion only. It is not at all necessary that she be John's assistant. We will find someone else. My reason for contacting Drake is to offer him a career comeback."

Tagee's attitude suddenly seemed to change, and after a moment he said, "That different. He make good money, hey?"

"Very good," Bonner said. "He would be able to live well, better then he ever has. And you can see how this would be a boon for your sister. She would be sharing in his good fortune."

"Even she don't be in act?"

"Right."

"How about me?" Tagee said. "You find job for me with your show?"

Bonner smiled again. "If you can convince Drake to accept my offer, I probably can."

"What I do in that job?"

"Roustabout, most likely."

"Roustabout? What a roustabout he do?"

"Help set up tents and spectator seats. Load and unload wagons."

"Hell, you forget I been hero too?"

"What kind of work are you doing now?"

"I been mucker in mines. Shovel ore in mine cars."

"Roustabouting is better than that. And you would travel with the show. Be with Drake and your sister."

"All right," Tagee said. "I take."

"You will have to get Drake to sign on with us first."

Tagee turned to Drake. "You going to sign?"

"No," Drake said.

Frustrated, Bonner left Antelope Wells on the next stage out.

His last words to Drake were "I'll be in Goldfield for a few days, scouting it out as a possible stop when we open our Nevada tour. I'll be staying at the new Casey Hotel briefly. Send word there if you change your mind."

When he left, he was no longer smiling.

Drake continued to wear the lawman's badge.

Whatever Henie's feelings were about the major's offer, she kept them hidden, making no further reference to it.

Tagee continued to work as a mucker, having only sporadic contact with either Drake or Henie. His only comment to her when he heard of Bonner's leaving was to say, "I think to be a roustabout better than what I do now. More better money maybe. But after get my part reward, I go back to work my claim anyway, I think."

CHAPTER 13

IN GOLDFIELD, AMONG the many fringe characters who made up part of the swollen population, was a boastful two-gun show-off who talked and acted as if he had just stepped from the pages of a Beadle and Adams dime novel. An ex-cowboy named Simon Cox.

As a matter of fact he had worked briefly as a hireling to keep sheepherders off the rancher's graze up in the northern part of the state. During this period he was involved in a couple of controversial shootings that resulted in the wounding of trespassing herders. And both times he had been brought to trial by sheep interests. These events had given him a public image to nurture: *Si Cox, gunfighter.*

For at each trial he had gone free on a plea of self-defense, the verdict rendered by juries composed of cowmen. The winning argument had been that the sheepherders had intruded where they shouldn't have. The way the juries saw it, the victims, though allegedly unarmed, had only got what was coming to them.

Despite his acquittals, he was not rehired by the ranching interests.

And so he had drifted down to Goldfield to try to exploit his reputation there.

And with a gun slung low on either hip he had bragged his way into a job as bodyguard to a newly rich mine-stock speculator, James Brogden.

He was a rather impressive figure—medium height, buckaroo lean of build, with still-young features set off by a long black mustache that slanted down on either jowl.

115

Despite being thirty, he gave the impression of coming from an older generation of legendary characters who had lived by the gun. It was obvious to some that he worked hard at projecting this.

But most of those who came in contact with him seemed to take him at face value, and it appeared that in the employ of the successful Brogden he had found a niche.

Had he reached Goldfield two years earlier he might have encountered the legendary Wyatt and Virgil Earp, main players in the 1881 shootout at the OK Corral in Tombstone.

The Earps, in a year-and-a-half stay, Virgil working as a security guard and Wyatt as a pit boss in a saloon, old men by then, had elicited possibly less attention than the flamboyant Cox did now.

Virgil had died of pneumonia in 1905, and Wyatt had left soon after for Los Angeles.

Ironically, neither one had cut nearly the figure during their stay that Si Cox, self-touted gunfighter, was doing.

A former sheepman down from Elko country knew of Cox's real background and resented it. Shortly after his arrival, while drinking in Tex Rickard's Northern Saloon, he encountered the owner and editor of a new newspaper struggling against the established two, the *Sun* and the *Chronicle*.

The newsman and the sheepman struck up a conversation that eventually found its way to the topic of Si Cox.

The newsman knew a story when he had one, and a couple of days later he had a sold-out edition when he ran an exposé of Cox's real gun experience.

The story effected an immediate change in the attitude of Cox's admirers.

Cox's first reaction was a desire to seek out the news editor and pistol-whip him, then find out the editor's information source and do the same to him.

But whatever he was, he wasn't a fool and quickly realized such actions would solve nothing for him, apart from satisfying his rage.

His boss, Brogden, had also read the story and had called him into his office. Brogden, seated behind a desk in his ornate office, said nothing at first, reaching out only to silently hand him a final paycheck.

Cox glanced at it. It was a full one. One thing you could say for the speculator, he had paid him well.

Cox's only thought was that he was going to miss this from here on.

Brogden said then, "I'm sorry, Cox, but your worth to me has lost its value."

"You believe that story in that stinking rag?"

"Whether I believe it or not makes little difference. Most of the townsfolk do and that's what counts."

Cox was silent.

Brogden went on. "There have been vague rumors now and then along the same lines. But as long as they were only rumors, they did not appreciably affect the protection you were able to give me. The threat of your reputation was strong enough to counter them."

"Suppose I told you the story is a lie?" Cox said.

Brogden stared at him, then said, "Are you listening to what I've been saying?"

When Cox did not answer, he went on, "If I were you, I'd look for some way to counteract the damage that's been done to you."

"How?" Cox said.

"Try to find a way to prove to the skeptics that you're still a man to reckon with. After all, you did shoot up several sheepherders." Brogden paused. "You'll have to find some other action elsewhere."

He had to get out of town. The changed attitude toward him was more than Cox's ego could tolerate.

He considered Brogden's suggestion. Go to where some action was and get involved in it. An incident or two, if handled right, could do it. Maybe even one.

Look at what had happened to that trick shot, John Drake.

The major newspapers carried periodically and favorably those incidents he handled there in Antelope Wells.

He'd met Drake when he was at the Hippodrome, although he'd not seen him perform.

Drake and Antelope Wells stayed in his mind, gave him an idea.

He'd go there.

Joad watched his passengers load into his stage.

He particularly noted Cox, whom he knew by sight and also by his somewhat picturesque garb, including the low-slung pair of six-guns.

The guns impressed him. If it were me, he thought, and after the word that has gone around Goldfield, I wouldn't have the balls to wear them. But I ain't him, he told himself, and I reckon that's the difference.

Cox seemed to sense his stare and met it with a cold one of his own.

Still an arrogant bastard, Joad thought, and then: I wonder how arrogant he'd be in a face-off with John Drake?

It was a thought that was to stick with him all the way to the Wells.

Especially after Cox asked to ride up on the box with him.

Joad weighed his request, and concluded it was Cox's wish to get away from the four other passengers, at least one or two of whom must have heard or read of Cox's loss of image.

Curious, Joad said, "Climb up."

Cox settled himself on the seat but did not further speak for several miles.

When he finally did, it was to ask a question.

"You acquainted with the constable at Antelope?"

"I've talked to him several times," Joad said.

"Become pretty famous lately, ain't he?"

"No more than his due," Joad said.

"Likes lawdogging, I guess."

Joad shrugged. "To him, it's just a job, that's all."

"Kind of a big comedown moneywise though, I'd guess. After him being in theatre business."

"I suppose so."

"I wonder would he want to get out of it?"

"I couldn't say," Joad said. "Personally, I wish he would."

"I might be able to arrange that," Cox said.

Joad gave him a sharp look. This was akin to what had been bothering him ever since he saw Cox waiting to board the coach.

In Antelope Wells, Drake was on the street as the stage pulled in at the hotel where it regularly stopped.

He glanced up at Joad and saw Si Cox seated alongside him.

Cox met his glance and held it for a significant moment before he began his climb down. As he reached the ground, Drake approached him.

Joad, still on the box, said, "How are you doing, John?"

"Well enough," Drake said. He paused, then said, "You got a man riding shotgun guard this trip, Joad?"

Cox spoke up quickly. "Drake, I never needed a shotgun." He slapped a hand on either hip-slung Colt. "Only these."

"Matter of speaking," Drake said. "How are you, Cox?"

Joad, setting the coach brake, said, "He wasn't riding guard, John. He chose to be a topside passenger."

"Some do," Drake said, and turned to let his eyes sweep over the other debarking passengers.

He turned back to Cox. "You here on Jim Brogden's business, Si?"

"Why do you ask that?"

"Job I've got here, I kind of like to know what's going on."

"I'm here on my own," Cox said. "A man can get tired of what he's doing. I been hearing a lot about Antelope Wells lately, thought I'd come look it over."

"Place is growing, all right," Drake said.

"I was surprised to hear you was wearing a star here," Cox said. "Kind of out of your line, ain't it?"

"Well, that's true."

"Big as the place is getting, it might be too much for you pretty soon."

"What does that mean, Si?"

"I was meaning for one man alone," Cox said. "Town this size sometimes needs a day constable and a night constable. But I guess you know that."

"Yeah, I know."

Joad had been standing nearby after helping the other passengers disembark, and catching the gist of the conversation, he interrupted.

"John, I'd like a word with you after I take the team to the station."

"I'll ride over with you."

With the team in the hands of the station stock tenders, Joad said to Drake, "I guess you haven't heard about Cox."

"Nothing new," Drake said. "But I guess he lost his job with Brogden."

"That's right. And I wanted to tell you why before he got your ear." Joad paused. "Or worse."

"Worse?"

"Let me give you the whole story," Joad said.

"I'd like to hear."

Joad spelled out the details. He ended up with, "Watch him, John. A character like him can be unpredictable."

Drake nodded. "I understand. He's been living on his pride. A false pride, but still something to live on. Now he's lost it. Could make him desperate."

"My thought exactly," Joad said.

The original ad hoc commitee of four who had hired Drake as constable—Whitside, the liveryman; Kunz, the mercantile owner; Goss, the barkeep; and Klessig, the hotelman—had expanded.

Two other business owners had been added, to form a town council of six. During the week after his arrival, Cox pitched his case to be made night lawman to each one.

It was Whitside who called them to meeting to consider the proposal, when it was brought up by Klessig. Drake's presence was also requested. Whitside was almost certain that Si Cox had talked the hotel owner into it.

Whitside opened the meeting by stating its purpose, which they all knew already.

"The decision to be made, is should we hire a second man to help John Drake enforce the law.

"As you know, Drake is on duty long hours each day, and now, as the town has grown, we are starting to have a problem with crimes occurring during late night. Not too many, but they are on the increase. Burglaries, muggings, holdups, and the like. Drake is doing a commendable job, but there is a limit to the hours he can put in.

"A town this size frequently requires a night constable to take over when the day constable's tour is over."

Whitside paused, then said, "Let's have your opinions on this matter."

There was a short silence.

Whitside said then, "Klessig, you seemed favorable to this hiring. Give us your argument why."

"Later," Klessig said. "Let some of these others begin."

Whitside frowned, then nodded. "All right."

Goss, the saloon keeper, spoke up. "I'll start—by objecting. I don't know how many of you have heard about the news story on Cox last week. It turns out his reputation as a gunman was a fraud."

"And how do you know that?" Whitside said.

"Them passengers that came last week on the same stage with him. They was from Goldfield where the story broke a few days before. Couple of them was in my place for a drink and told me all about it."

Whitside looked over the listeners and said, "How many of you have heard this."

Kunz said, "I think maybe all of us have heard a rumor, at least. But let's have it from Goss."

Goss said, "A fellow from up Elko way knew Cox up there. And Cox's reputation, it turns out, is mostly big-mouth."

"Tell us what you heard," Whitside said.

Goss did exactly that.

Most of the others nodded as he went along.

When he'd finished, Whitside said, "I heard pretty much the same thing from Joad, the stage driver, whom I trust. It seems to me that Cox is here in the hope of re-establishing himself, despite a spotty record. I am not very impressed with his qualifications for the job. But I believe, as I said earlier, that the town has grown to where Drake needs some help."

Klessig spoke up then.

"Exactly. I've talked to Cox, and he impressed on me that he was the victim of some bastard up north who bad-mouthed him to a struggling newspaper owner needing a headline story." Klessig paused, then said, "I say give Cox a chance to prove himself. If that's a mistake, we can fire him."

Whitside said, "Drake? What do you say?"

"If he's to be only on a night tour, I'm agreeable."

"Let's have a vote then," Whitside said.

Goss was the only one dissenting.

A week went by with the new arrangement.

And having a night constable seemed to have its effect.

There was only a single burglary reported—of a residence.

It seemed that even if some word of Cox's diminished image had spread, the criminal element was not too eager to test it.

Drake was pleased, having only one reservation: the burglary had not been reported to him by Cox, but by the victim.

Drake then hunted up Cox to discuss what he felt was a point to be resolved.

He'd said, "Si, I want to be informed of any lawbreaking incident that occurs during your shift."

Cox said, "I didn't think you'd want to be bothered."

More likely he wanted to hide the fact that it had occurred while he was on duty, Drake thought.

But all he said was "From now on you know differently."

Cox made no reply.

"You understand?" Drake said.

"Drake," Cox said, "don't be using tall tones on me."

"I don't intend to," Drake said. "I'm just asking a simple question."

"All right," Cox said, and turned away.

A few more days passed.

When Cox replaced Drake at midnight or when he ended his tour at noon, they usually met at the improvised office.

There was little said between them.

Drake only made it routine to ask, "Any trouble to report?"

So far Cox had always given the same answer, "Nothing."

Drake was curious about this at first, but finally decided that a stronger vestige of Cox's reputation still existed here than it apparently had in Goldfield.

If Cox hadn't seen fit to bring in anybody to the lockup, he must be keeping things under control, even in the eastern part of town. This was an area of late-night saloons, gambling layouts, and whore's cribs. But Cox seemed to be handling it even as Drake had done. By strength of reputation.

Cox had sensed at once that he could not let the denizens of the tenderloin adopt the attitude that the Goldfield populace had done. He could not let it take a foothold here.

From the day Cox put on the badge, he walked the rough streets with heavy boots. He'd made a career of acting a hardcase, and he played the role here with a vengeance.

And it seemed, soon enough, to be working.

And that is how he came to pistol-whip unconscious a young rambunctious drunken miner he encountered in a crowded saloon. The kid was standing at the bar and relating loudly what he'd heard about the Cox fiasco as he called it. The bartender tried to shut him up, but Cox himself came in the door in time to hear.

"Acts like a curly wolf, don't he? Curly-wolf Cox, he'd like to be called," the young miner was saying, facing the bar.

Cox kept approaching, and the miner kept talking.

"Curly wolf—hell! Damn fourflusher is what he is."

Cox's hand grabbed his shoulder and spun him around.

The miner's eyes squinted drunkenly, trying to focus on Cox's face, then dropped to stare at the badge pinned on Cox's coat.

"Curly wolf's badge," he said.

"Let's step outside, kid," Cox said.

"Hell, yes," the kid said, not really knowing what he was saying.

Cox pushed him, stumbling and staggering, through the crowd and out onto the street.

Once there, he spun him around, drew his right-hand gun, and started belaboring him with its barrel. Not too hard at first, but with fast, quick blows to the jowls and neck and shoulders that ripped and smashed the flesh. Within seconds the kid's face was a bloody mess.

The kid did not cry out or even try to protect himself, too stunned by the attack to do either. He just stood there and took it until Cox tired of his effort and measured him for two swinging smashes against the temple that dropped him. He lay there in the dust, eyes closed and unmoving.

Cox turned his attention then to that part of the crowd who had managed to exit the saloon doorway.

One of them was cursing and moved out from the others as if to better see the inert kid.

"Stay where you are," Cox said, looking at him.

The man stopped and said, "Might be he's dead."

"Might be he is," Cox said. "If so, there ain't much you can do for him, is there."

The man met Cox's eyes and swallowed hard. "No, I reckon not."

He moved back to where the others were standing, and attempted to push his way back into the saloon.

He kept saying, "Dammit! let me through. I need a drink."

Cox said to the others, "Let him lay, you hear?"

The kid wasn't dead. But he did lie there awhile before he got to his feet and staggered off to his shack where he slept. He had trouble even finding it in the dark, and in his condition.

Once there, he passed out again and slept fretfully while darkness gave way to dawn and beyond.

He awoke finally in midmorning, sick with a hangover and the pain of the beating. But his thinking was surprisingly clear in recalling what had happened. That he had stood helpless while a badge-wearing son of a bitch beat him into oblivion.

Despite his sickness, a wild rage surged within him. A

hate for that night marshal who had started to throw his weight around.

If he had the chance, he would kill the bastard.

Kill the bastard, he began to repeat to himself, over and over.

Rummaging in a clothes bag, he found the old beat-up Smith and Wesson revolver he'd won in a poker game months before.

He spun the cylinder and saw it was loaded.

Next thing he knew, he'd shoved it into the waistband of his trousers, pulled out his shirttail to cover it, and went out unsteadily into the town, thinking to prowl until he found that badge toter.

Give him a taste of his own medicine.

Constable Drake was alone in the office, bringing up to date a journal he was logging of his law-keeping incidents, all minor during this period.

It was a little early for him to even be here. It was a couple of hours yet before his tour began at noon.

The thought occurred to him that he might wander the town off-duty just to see how things were going with his alternate.

Presently he was doing just that, having saddled his horse with the intention of riding over to the tenderloin.

The kid wandered aimlessly in the hot sun. The ache in his head was worse. He was having blinding flashes of white light every few minutes, like silent explosions inside his skull.

Each time it left him with darkened vision as if he were trying to see at night.

Staggering to the side of the street, he sat on a stoop in front of an unoccupied wood structure.

He could not remember where he was or why.

Then he saw the man on the horse coming toward him from the west, sun glinting on a piece of metal on his chest.

It came back to him then. A badge toter. On a horse now, but there he was.

Coming toward him.

Coming back to beat him some more.

The kid reached his hand inside his shirt and closed it on the butt of his gun.

Si Cox had turned onto the street and was walking westward when he saw Drake, mounted and riding easily toward him.

He also saw the figure sitting on the stoop midway between.

Even though he was twenty yards away, Cox could see the splatter of dried blood on his clothing and recognized him as the bigmouthed kid he had beaten several hours before.

Cox drew one of his guns as he moved toward him.

He could see now that the kid was unaware of his approach as he watched Drake ride closer.

Cox was ten yards from the kid, and Drake twice that distance in the other direction, when the kid raised a gun and fired at Drake.

Cox blew the back of the kid's head away with a single shot.

He looked beyond and saw the blood staining Drake's shoulder. Drake was clinging with his left hand to the horn of his saddle.

Cox grinned. Damnfool kid, he thought. Couldn't do anything right. Shot the wrong man.

CHAPTER 14

WITH THE INCREASED activity in the town, Doc Ramsey had returned to Antelope Wells, seeking a spot to open an office. Unable to find a place available, he had rented a tent behind the hotel and let word of mouth carry the news of his presence.

So it was to Doc Ramsey that Drake made his way with his wound.

Ramsey looked at him and said, "I heard you were lawdogging here now. But I didn't expect you to be my first patient."

"I didn't expect to be," Drake said. "This wound isn't too serious."

"A layman's opinion," Doc said. "They're all serious if infection sets in."

"I'm hoping you'll prevent that."

"Let's get your shirt off and see."

Ramsay examined a deep graze wound on Drake's right shoulder.

"You're damn lucky this time," Ramsey said. "Not much worse than the one your Paiute partner had in that other gunplay."

"Glad to hear that, doctor."

"Yes," Ramsey said. "Lucky. As you were in the earlier fight with that other gunman you killed in the dark."

"You heard about that?"

"Of course. Everything that happens to you makes the news."

Drake was silent.

"What are you doing wearing that badge, anyway?" Doc said. "Sooner or later your luck will run out. It's happened to lesser-knowns. But you're a prize target for any fool looking for quick fame. I had believed the day of the gunfighter was over, but Nevada's new activity at Tonopah and Goldfield has brought out a fringe of latter-day want-to-be's."

It was Ramsey's turn to be silent then, as he went to work cleansing and bandaging the wound.

When he'd finished, he said, "That shoulder will be sore for a while. Let me warn you against getting into any immediate armed confrontations. Your dexterity may be greatly handicapped." He paused. "And I'll give you some other heartfelt advice: Give up that law badge. Find some other way to make a living."

"What other way?" Drake said.

Ramsey hesitated, then said, "Resume your career. Make a fresh start."

"That's easy to say, Doctor. But I'm not sure it's possible to do."

"I know. You've heard of my own career failures, I'm sure. I left Goldfield because of them. But, in a way, I'm here now to make a comeback. Why? Because medicine is what I know."

"There's a difference, Doctor. In my case I was involved, as you witnessed, in a mistake that resulted in a death."

Ramsey did not reply at once. Then he said, "I will not give you details of something I'm trying to forget. But I too have made mistakes in my career. One, that like yours, resulted in a death. An accidental slip of a surgeon's knife. I let guilt drive me to refuge in liquor. But now I'm making a new try."

"Your case is some different than mine," Drake said.

"Some, yes. But the similarities are there." Doc paused. "For what they're worth. But think about what I'm saying."

"I will," Drake said.

*   *   *

He returned to his residence, his arm temporarily in a sling, his shirt blood-stained at the sleeve.

Henie immediately took notice.

She met his eyes but did not speak.

"Minor wound," he said.

"And your attacker?"

"Dead."

"But it could have gone the other way," she said.

It was not a point he could argue.

"Two men, two guns," she said. "A fifty-fifty chance for either."

He was still silent. Cox's critical part in that bothered him.

"How many times until it goes the other way, John?"

He shrugged and winced at the pain that caused. And thought of what Doc Ramsey had just said to him.

Drake went to his office and found Whitside there. The liveryman eyed his shoulder.

"I ran into Ramsey on the street and heard what happened."

"Yes?"

"I've got to talk to you, John."

"About this?" Drake said, touching the sling with his left hand.

"I know now it was a mistake for me and the others to ask you to take on the lawman job. We thought your reputation would keep the rowdy element in line. And it pretty well has."

Drake waited.

The ostler paused, then went on. "What none of us reckoned with was the danger all this publicity has brought you."

"It did not occur to me either," Drake said.

"It seems to me now there is only one way to end the risk

that fame has brought you. That's to take that badge away from you. We'll find some unknown to wear it—just the opposite of what we've tried before." Whitside paused. "Or, hell, let Cox take over."

"There's just one thing," Drake said. "I'm depending on that lawman's pay now for subsistence."

Whitside hesitated before saying, "There was a rumor heard that a stranger hanging around a few days and seen talking with you was in show business. Is that so?"

"Yes, that's true."

"Did he make you any kind of an offer?"

"Matter of fact he did."

"Maybe you should accept it," the liveryman said. "Under the circumstances."

He did not patrol the rest of that day, nor the next. On the third day, with the sling removed, he began his rounds again, but with trepidation. The soreness of the wound had stiffened most of the muscles in his arm and he knew by trial before leaving home that he would be slow and awkward in handling his weapon.

He had stepped outside to avoid Henie watching him, but she was not fooled by the ruse.

"Don't go, John," she said. "Please don't go."

"I'll be all right," he said. "It's not likely I'll be accosted this soon after what happened."

"You don't know that. Turn in your badge. Please!"

"I'm giving it some strong thought."

"Do it now!"

He did not speak again for a long moment. Then he said, "I know I'm not cut out to wear the star. Still, I have posed as one who is, and foolish as it may be, I have taken a measure of pride in it. To abruptly quit now, because of what amounts to hardly more than a scratch, goes counter to that pride. Can you understand that?"

"No, I cannot," she said.

He frowned.

"I will make my rounds today, at least," he said. And left.

Late in the day, Joad pulled in again with the stage.

Drake had returned to his office, having made his tour without mishap, and presently the driver made an appearance there.

His first words to Drake were "By god! I no more than got here and somebody told me you'd took a bullet again from some other yahoo!"

"I ended up with a scratch."

"I heard the details. Enough to know it's time you quit."

"I'm thinking of it."

"I got information that may help your thinking," Joad said. "The reward money came through on those convicts. Sheriff Will Ingalls is holding it for your pickup in Goldfield."

"He could have sent it."

"Department of Prisons check, I reckon. Sizable amount and no bank here to cash it, he probably figured."

"True."

"Bit of other news, too. Fellow named Major Bonner sends word that he's about to leave Goldfield. Said to tell you he'll wait for the stage return to hear your decision on his offer. He's got to rejoin his show someplace in California."

Drake considered this without comment.

After a pause, Joad said, "A Wild West show that figures to kick off a Nevada tour next month in Reno."

"Reno?" Drake said.

"He told me you could be a featured act with them," Joad said.

Again Drake was silent.

"None of my business," Joad said. "But, John, it sounds like you could have a real future there."

Drake appeared deeply thoughtful for a spell.

Then he said, "Put me down as a passenger tomorrow to Goldfield."

"You're going to sign on for the show?"

"I'm going to get the reward money," Drake said.

On the long stage ride to his destination, accompanied by two mining engineers who were discouraged by his laconic response to their attempts to maintain conversation with him, Drake remained deep in thought.

He disembarked in Goldfield in front of the Palace Saloon, the bottom floor of a two-story stone structure. The upper floor contained the office of Sheriff Ingalls.

The sheriff was in neither the saloon nor his office, but an elderly clerk recognized and greeted Drake.

"I came for the reward on those two escaped convicts," Drake said.

"Yes, of course, sir," the clerk said. He went to a corner floor safe, opened it, and came back with a check.

"Will you be staying again in Goldfield, Mr. Drake?"

"It is not my intention," Drake said.

The clerk nodded. "I can understand, sir," he said.

Drake made his way to the Casey Hotel, where Bonner had said he would be staying.

The hotel, newly constructed, was elaborately designed with a lobby music stand, elevator, and thirty-six suites with private baths.

The major, Drake was thinking, was inclined toward the best available.

The desk man sent word up to his suite, informing him of Drake's presence.

Drake moved across the lobby to sit in one of the luxurious lounge chairs.

Goldfield, he thought, must have just about reached its peak if there were investors anteing up funds for buildings such as this.

A few minutes later, Bonner stepped out of the elevator. As he approached, Drake stood to shake his hand.

Bonner smiled only slightly. He appeared concerned about what Drake might be about to say.

"You've made a decision?" he said.

Drake nodded. "Yes. But with conditions."

"And what are they?"

"That Henie will not be assisting in my act."

"I said we'd find someone else."

"And that you give Tagee a job with the show, as you mentioned to him before."

"If that's what he wants."

"I'm not certain that he does—but if it is."

"Agreed."

"You have a contract ready?"

"Yes. I presume the weekly salary I offered is satisfactory?"

"Yes."

Bonner withdrew the document from a briefcase he carried, and handed it to Drake to read.

When Drake finished and nodded, the major said, "We can sign it over there at the registration desk. The clerk can be witness to our signatures."

As they moved in that direction, Drake said, "I've heard you intend to start the Nevada tour in Reno."

"Tentatively yes."

"You considered earlier it might be here."

"Possibly later. But Reno provides more accessibility on the Central Pacific main rail line. We are currently showing in northern California and have to ship across the Sierras. It's a matter of logistics."

"I notice this contract becomes effective when I join up."

"The crossing is imminent, and you will start when we unload at our destination. Possibly in a week. Do you need a salary advance?"

"No, I've just received the reward money from the state prison authority."

"Very well," Bonner said. "I'll get word to you when we reach Reno, and you can join us then."

Drake was thoughtful, then said, "Major, you are in show business. You realize, of course, that I have to work out a performing routine and rehearse it. Although several years ago I began my career in a small Wild West show, it is imperative that I be totally prepared."

"Yes, I am quite aware of that," Bonner said. "And we will not feature you in our advertising for our first week after we relocate. That will give you time."

"Reno," Drake said, "is a prominent city, by Nevada standards. But its population isn't likely to warrant a long stay there."

"You are forgetting the other towns within reach. Carson City, Virginia City," Bonner said. "And by the time you are ready we will be spreading the word by every means available that you are again performing as the featured act of *Winston's*. We are banking on the power of your draw, my boy. We believe you'll even draw people from outlying ranches and mining communities." He paused. "And then, of course, we will be moving on with our projected tour."

"I see," Drake said. "We will be waiting then to hear from you."

"We? Do you mean you and that Paiute, Tagee?"

"I don't know for certain what Tagee will choose to do. I was speaking of myself and Henie. You knew, of course, that she will be with me wherever I go?"

"Of course, of course," the major said. "And her being Indian, we just might work her into the show."

Winston's Wild West gave a final performance in Sacramento, California, and began to load its conglomeration of animals, wagons, props, knockdown audience bleachers, and sundry other articles onto the freight cars of the Central Pacific.

It was a monumental effort, yet one that progressed with relative smoothness, perfected on repeated prior occasions.

Last to board, and into passenger cars, were the staff and performers and those roustabouts not delegated to ride with the freight.

Hal Winston and his staff rode in a car by themselves.

Major Bonner had rejoined them.

Among the others were George Bourke, general manager; Jake Kane, treasurer; Wesley Walden, business manager; Harry Farr, superintendent; and Frank Riley, press agent.

Bonner's title was advance agent, usually working ahead in preparation of sites and advertising displays, and also on occasion, booking an outstanding talent.

He now formally announced Drake's booking, although the word had already spread to the others.

Hal Winston was a big man, over six feet and two hundred pounds, with a physique that in his younger years had easily landed him a job as a circus roustabout in New York State.

From there he had worked in various capacities with the circus, including a brief stint as its general manager, before it went bankrupt.

Yet he had somehow managed to get investors to back a show of his own, only this time patterned on that of Buffalo Bill Cody.

He believed he would find a near virgin market in the West and was willing to gamble on it.

He hedged his bet a little by first shipping his show to Los Angeles, beginning a tour that worked up through California with fair success until it reached the so-called cow counties of the north.

There, in cattle country, he was doubly pleased by the eager reception he encountered.

It strengthened his earlier conviction that he would find his show might have great popularity in what remained of the real West. And led to his decision to cross the Sierra to once-again-booming Nevada.

Now he congratulated Bonner again for his signing on of John Drake.

"One thing," the major said. "We have to find a suitable assistant for his performance."

Harry Farr, the show superintendent, said to Winston, "Hal, we've got an ambitious young roustabout working for us who tells me he's had some summer-stock acting experience. He just might jump at the chance to assist Drake."

"Ambitious, eh? Did you know I began like that myself—only with a circus?"

"So I heard," Farr said, just as if he hadn't heard it too many times. It was a fact that Hal Winston was proud of.

"Send him around to see me when we get to Reno," Winston said.

"Right," Farr said. "Will do."

They crossed the formidable High Sierras on the spectacular rail route and unloaded the show and set it up on a site previously selected by Bonner.

The major, immediately on reaching their destination, sent word to Drake of their arrival: *Come at once to begin rehearsals. Have an assistant for your act. Bonner.*

Drake, Henie, and Tagee caught the next stage out, which now ran every other day to Goldfield. From there they caught the train to Reno.

Tagee had told Drake he'd decided to try his luck with the show, but had given no other reason.

Since Tagee had his share of the reward money he could

have gone back to working his claim. Drake guessed he had decided to become a roustabout to watch over the welfare of his sister.

As soon as Drake, Henie, and Tagee arrived, they were given copies of the show's program of events.

Drake read it with interest, noting the similarities to the show with which he had toured earlier.

First of the events was *Overture: The Star Spangled Banner*, played by a cowboy band.

Then came a review of riders in cavalry uniforms who were billed as the *Rough Riders of the Recent Spanish-American War*.

Next was *Floyd Harken, the Celebrated Rifle Shot*, who blasted glass balls thrown high into the air, firing from a variety of physical postures, including standing on his head.

He was followed by a group of young riders in *Pony Express* attire who raced around the arena demonstrating transfer of mail pouches and exchanges of mounts while being chased by whooping Indians.

And a *Covered Wagon Attack*, where marauding Indians were driven off by the rifle fire of a courageous husband and wife.

Cowboys demonstrating acrobatic *Feats of Horsemanship*.

Mexicans from Old Mexico showing their own style of *Riding and Roping Tricks*.

Cowboys Riding Bucking Horses.

Another exhibition of glass-ball shooting, this time by *The Woman Rifle Champion, Elsie Baxter*.

Capture of a Stagecoach by Indians in full war regalia, its occupants rescued by a small detachment of cavalry led by Hal Winston hemself, magnificent in army scout buckskins.

These were some of the highlights of the show.

With the show sited on the selected grounds, *Winston's*

drew a quite satisfactory crowd for its first performances. As word spread of its exciting and novel presentations, ensuing performances were expected to bring increased crowds of spectators seeking to vicariously relive the legendary thrills of the recent frontier past.

Drake was wondering where he would fit into the program, and he asked Bonner.

"We're giving you a featured spot," the major said. "We will listen to your suggestions."

Drake had given this some thought, and now he said, "My own choice would be just before the grand finale, when all the performers parade across the arena in front of the crowd."

Bonner nodded. "Sounds fine to me," he said. "Winston will make the decision though."

"And now," Drake said, "who is going to be my assistant?"

"I'll bring him to you," Bonner said.

A short time later he reappeared with a well-built young man in roustabout clothes.

"John, this is Gilbert Castle, who has volunteered to play second lead in your performance." Bonner grinned. "I put it that way because he has had theatrical stage experience. Gilbert, this is John Drake."

Castle reached out a hand, which Drake took, and said, "I will do my best for you, Mr. Drake."

He had the looks for a leading man, Drake thought, and could well have stage presence. But would he be up to the role he would be required to handle when the bullets flew?

Bonner said, "We've procured the equipment and props we think you'll need. And I would ask, John, that you begin rehearsing at once. We want to get you before our audience in as few days as possible."

The rehearsals began the next morning. They were planned to continue each day at the same hour, prior to show time.

Drake and Castle began with a run-through of his familiar routine, but done dry without any actual shooting.

It was a routine that ran approximately a half hour, even without actual use of guns.

It was quickly apparent that Castle was familiar with stage directions, and he had an excellent awareness of small bits of business that could serve to embellish an act.

Drake was well pleased with these first run-throughs.

That first morning they went through the motions of the act several times.

Drake said to Castle, "It went well. You learn quickly."

"Thanks," Castle said.

"Tomorrow we'll try some of the easier shooting."

"Fine."

Later Drake kept recalling Castle's ready reply of "Fine."

It bothered him, not because of the way Castle so readily said it, but because Drake wasn't at all that sure his own reply would have been likewise.

After Castle left for his own quarters, Henie said, "He did well, didn't he? And now I've seen what your act is all about."

"Not quite all," Drake said. "You'll see some of that tomorrow."

"It's something I'm looking forward to," she said.

He took that in silence.

She studied him closely then, and said, "You can do it, John."

"Sure," he said.

CHAPTER 15

JACK SHAW'S GUN arm was gone, below what had been the midpoint between his shoulder and elbow. There was just a stub remaining.

He could have felt some gratitude that he had always been reasonably ambidextrous and could make more use of his left arm than some men could. But there was no gratitude in him. Just hate for the man who'd made the amputation necessary.

He knew now who that was.

He knew from reading the news accounts of the shootings.

Buck Lemon had read them, too. Buck was giving him room and board, for old times' sake, while he convalesced. The old man sympathized with him and could put himself in Shaw's place and understand his feeling.

That's why Buck furnished him with a gun and bought him bullets to practice left-hand shooting.

All thought of a future had left Shaw. He no longer cared what lay ahead. Gone was his idea of reaching Arizona and maybe going straight.

He sometimes thought of the Paiute girl and the hope he'd had of keeping her with him in a new life. It was something he could still savor, although he now knew it could never be realized.

Most of his time was spend in a secluded, improvised firing range far back of Buck's hotel. There he slowly acquired dexterity with his left arm and hand.

Strangely, as his proficiency with his left-hand shooting

141

increased, so did the frequency of his fantasizing about the girl.

He reached a point where his contemplation of *what might have been* became *what still might be.*

And in his mind he grew more and more certain that she would have willingly taken up with him had not that bastard Drake interfered. It was one more reason to settle the score.

Then one day Buck Lemon came out to the firing range to see how he was doing.

Buck watched him for a while and said, "You look about ready, Jack."

"I been thinking the same thing," Shaw said.

"The last I read about him," Buck said, "he was still law-dogging as constable up in Antelope Wells."

"As good a place as any for me to do what I aim to do," Shaw said.

Buck hesitated, then said, "One thing to remember, Jack. They say he's had two showdowns with would-be gun slicks up there."

"I know," Shaw said.

"You know then that they're dead, and he's still walking the streets."

"I figure to end that," Shaw said.

"All right, Jack," Buck said. "I've done what I can for you. Your horse has got good care at the livery. Ready for the trip."

"I'll need a few bucks for when I get there," Shaw said.

"I'll spare you that too," Buck said. "For old times' sake." He paused. "I miss them times, now and then."

"Looking back," Shaw said, "in some ways they was the best."

"For sure," Buck said.

Following the trail that would take him back to the Wells, Shaw sometimes saw his own old tracks, not yet oblit-erated by wind and sand. His memory of the agony he had undergone at that time fed his rage now. A rage that needed no feeding.

He pictured in his mind how he would face-off that son of a bitch who had taken his arm.

Maybe he would hold up the stump and let the bastard see it good before he triggered a volley of shots into his gut.

A gut-shot Drake would die in agony.

While he, Shaw, stood and watched. Enjoying it.

His enjoyment of the imagined scene was short as his mind brought him back to reality. Hell, you couldn't give a damn trick shot, like they said Drake was, a warning.

The sensible way to do it was to bushwhack him.

Maybe shoot him in the back. Play it safe.

That was the practical way, Shaw thought. But he knew it would never satisfy the rage that burned within him.

He would have to let the dirty rotten bastard know who was killing him.

His mind made up on that point, he rode for a spell at peace with himself.

Until he thought again of the girl.

That was when he came to the spot in the lava field where he had been forced to tie her up at the insistence of Longo and Huff.

He remembered how he had done so reluctantly, trying to explain it, even as he finally told her how he felt.

He recalled his words to her, when he'd said, *"I'm going to Arizona to start over. Free from the outlaw trail. I want you to stay with me. I want you to be with me when I go straight."*

And he remembered again, many miles later as he reached the place where the Joshuas grew heavily, where they had rested in the shade and he had taken her aside and first told her, *"I'm sorry for the rough treatment."*

And she had said, *"You are a strange man."*

"Maybe so," he'd said. *"But I never felt like this before. Not since maybe when I was real young."*

It had been true, what he'd told her.

And he rode for a long time with this in his mind.

Eventually he reached the Wells.

He had to be careful now, he knew. Even though he had grown a beard, there were people here who still might recognize him.

The liveryman for one. Possibly the tender at the saloon where they had stopped for a drink.

He was astonished at how much the town had grown since that time. Its population was three times what it had been, he guessed. And it was widely spread out from the small cluster of structures that had made up the town.

All the better for him. He could stay away from what had been the nucleus of the camp. There must be another livery on the fringe somewhere that would provide for his horse while he searched out information on Drake.

Despite the increased size of the place, that shouldn't take more than a day or so, he figured.

He stopped in one of the now many saloons and nursed a couple of drinks. After a while he struck up an idle conversation with the bartender.

"I just rode in. Heard the place has got kind of a famous constable here. I'm passing through and thought I'd like to see a guy made a name for hisself like it appears he done."

The barman looked Shaw over, scanning the range clothes that he was wearing. Shaw had bought them on Buck Lemon's account before he left Indian Springs.

"You come a couple days late for that," the barkeep said. "He ain't here no more. Left a couple days ago. Went to Reno. We heard he was hired on for a shooting act in one of them Buffalo Bill kind of shows."

"The hell you say!" Shaw said. His frustration showed.

The barman noted this and said, "You want to see him in action, the place would be up there."

"Reno, huh?" Shaw said then. "Yeah, I guess that would be the place to do it."

*   *   *

He sold his horse to a recently started livery across the town from where he and his former partners had stopped before.

He then paid to hitch a ride with a freighter leaving the Wells for Goldfield.

He had been letting his beard grow for a long time now and believed it disguised him enough that he would not be identified by some Wanted poster that might have been circulated so many weeks before.

In his pocket he still had money enough for rail fare from Goldfield to Reno, and to sustain himself there briefly.

Long enough to do what he had to do.

CHAPTER 16

THE REHEARSING OF Drake's act with Gilbert Castle went on for several days.

Henie watched it always, and Bonner did so on occasion.

A week passed, and the major questioned Drake's readiness to perform.

"Yes," Drake said, "I'm ready."

Bonner turned to Castle. "And you, Gilbert?"

Castle gave him a nod in answer, but there was a bit of concern on his face.

"Fine," the major said. "We have posters in living color, showing the two of you in eye-catching action. We're already posting them on fences and structures around Reno wherever we can."

Castle said, "I'd like to see one."

"You can," Bonner said. He had been holding a large roll of paper under his arm, and now he unrolled it.

Drake, Castle, and Henie all stared silently at it.

Then Drake said, "There's only one thing wrong with it."

"And what is that?" Bonner said.

"It shows me shooting an apple off Gilbert's head."

Bonner smiled. "Just like William Tell. It's Mr. Winston's idea. And get this: as you prepare to shoot, we'll have the band break out in the opening bars of the William Tell Overture."

"No!" Drake said.

"Why not?" The major's words were suddenly querulous. "The band's accompaniment is Mr. Winston's idea also."

"I don't mean no to the band," Drake said. "I mean no to the whole thing."

"Why?"

"Shooting toward a person holding an object to one side," Drake said, "even a cigarette or cigar in the mouth, can be disastrous if the shooter's aim is at fault— laterally—"

He stopped, momentarily unable to continue, thinking about Molly.

Then he said, "But shooting at a target on top of a person's head adds the danger that a weak primer in a cartridge could make the slug hit lower."

"God!" Gilbert Castle said.

Bonner frowned, annoyed by this revelation.

But Drake went on. "Low enough to strike the forehead instead of the apple."

"God!" Castle said again.

Bonner was silent, then said, "I'll tell Mr. Winston. But he is not going to like it."

He remained another moment, held by his reluctance to take Drake's refusal to the show boss. When he did leave, he moved slowly.

Drake frowned and exchanged glances with Castle. He saw the increased concern on the assistant's face.

Trying to ease that, he said, "Don't worry, Gilbert. I'll have no part of their plan."

"I'm glad you told the major so," Castle said. But he still looked worried.

"Something else bothering you?" Drake said.

"Well, yes. I'm bothered by what you said can happen if a shooter's aim is at fault, aside from the apple-on-the-head trick. Of course I knew about the danger and about what happened, uh, in Goldfield. But somehow I had pushed it out of my mind. Perhaps because I wanted to get back in front of an audience. Show business is my goal in life."

"And?"

"What you said about faulty aim brought it back with shocking impact."

"And now?"

"Well . . . it was a passing shock, that's all. I knew there was a possible risk in what I'd be doing, but I guess I figured it beat being a roustabout the rest of my life."

"You will continue then?"

"Yes," Castle said.

"Good," Drake said. But he didn't feel right in saying it.

Bonner reported back to Drake that Winston had agreed to halt distribution of the apple-trick poster. Those that had been pasted to fences or sides of structures would have to remain, of course. Only a long period of Nevada weathering would remove them.

Drake was bothered by the thought of disappointed ticket buyers, perhaps lured by the existing displays. If any of the show's staff shared this worry, they made no mention of it. Drake supposed that working in a business where exaggeration was pretty much the norm, they expected their audiences to tolerate a certain amount of it.

They finished their final rehearsal, but the last few tricks did not all go well.

Castle still looked nervous and this bothered Drake. What worried him more was that Gilbert gave a slight flinch on two occasions when Drake fired.

It made Drake miss both times.

"What's the problem, Gil?"

"I don't know," Castle said. "But I won't let it happen again."

"I hope not," Drake said. "You're making me look bad."

Their act went on before an audience in the matinee performance of the next day.

It went smoothly and drew great response.

The response quickly settled Castle into his role, just as it probably had when he was an actor.

Drake surprised himself at how easily he handled his own part of the routine. Shooting around a male target holder might have been part of the reason, he thought. There was nothing about the rugged ex-roustabout to remind him of Molly. And thank God for that.

Henie witnessed all this and was quick to compliment Drake, as well as Gilbert.

"I knew you could do it, John," she said when they were alone. "I was even more sure when I watched you rehearsing."

Winston was pleased at how well this new act was received. He came around personally to tell Drake so.

They played a few more days, and then Bonner brought a message from Winston of a change in plans.

"We're going to move on," the major said. "No reflection on you, John, but we've outstayed our market here. Your act has served to prolong it, but the take has dropped greatly as the people in this Reno area have been saturated. Too bad you had to spend time rehearsing, but you'll knock them dead in our next stop."

"And where will that be?"

"Mr. Winston has decided to take the show to Goldfield."

"Goldfield!"

"Second-biggest town in this part of Nevada," Bonner said. "And we can draw additional audience from Tonopah."

There had been other reasons discussed between the showman and Bonner regarding the choice of the new location. Among them was Winston's comment, "Listen, Major, Drake's act could pack them in at Goldfield because the whole town still remembers what happened at the Hippodrome."

"I agree," the major said.

"I know the public. A lot of people will attend on the unmentionable chance that Drake will miss again with tragic results!"

Bonner said, "That's the very thought I had from the beginning. Morbid interest can be great for increasing gate receipts."

"A hell of a thing," Winston said. "But true."

"Yes, it is."

Winston said then, "I've been giving a lot of thought to how we could squeeze even more advantage from this particular situation."

"And how is that?"

"If we could have a woman assistant for him, instead of Gilbert Castle."

"Who?" Bonner said.

"Didn't you tell me that Paiute girl has watched every rehearsal? And that she was once willing—even eager—to take the part?"

"I did. But Drake himself refused to let her."

"Then we have to make Drake change his mind," Winston said.

CHAPTER 17

JACK SHAW REACHED Goldfield via the freight wagon and caught a train bound for Reno. He carried his gun hidden in a small valise slung by a long strap from his shoulder.

He arrived there just as a train loaded with the Wild West Show was waiting on a siding, ready to leave.

By the time he had debarked and figured out what was happening, the train was pulling out on the track bound for where he had left so many long grinding hours before. It was now dusk.

He stood there staring after it, cursing his luck. Gaining no relief, he stormed into the depot and accosted the rail agent.

"Where the hell's that show headed?"

"Going to set up in Goldfield, I understand. Give the folks down there a treat."

"I just come up from there to see the show," Shaw said bitterly.

"Great show," the agent said. "Too bad you missed it. You want to see it, you'll have to make a return trip."

Shaw had counted his money on the train up and knew he lacked several dollars of the fare.

He had a strong impulse to pull his revolver and smash it over the agent's head but fought against it. He'd best not raise any hell that might further impede his mission.

He stomped out of the station, then turned and went back in.

The agent gave him a quizzical look and said, "You want that return ticket?"

"When does the next train leave?"

"Won't be one till tomorrow morning. Six o'clock."

That gave him all night to steal what he needed, Shaw thought.

"I'll see you then," he said. "I have to see a friend first."

The agent had heard those words before and guessed it meant Shaw lacked the price. He said again, "Great show. You go back there to see it, you'll get a lot of satisfaction out of some of the acts they put on."

"Yeah?"

"They got a trick shot doing his act, the one that used to perform in the Hippodrome Theatre there. Maybe you heard of him—the one who accidentally killed his woman on stage?"

"I bet he's something to see," Shaw said.

"If you ever tried any gun shooting, you'd appreciate the way he can do it. Either hand."

He stopped suddenly then, as if he'd just noticed Shaw's arm was missing.

"Sorry," he said, still staring at the stump.

Shaw thought fast. It might be well to have this fellow sympathetic toward him.

He said, "Don't be. I've had nine years to get used to it."

"Nine years?" the agent said. "That would make it in ninety-eight. The War year. Cuba, maybe?"

"Yeah," Shaw said. "Me and Teddy Roosevelt at San Juan Hill."

"Always a pleasure to meet a war hero," the agent said. "Listen, I'll hold a reservation for you for the morning departure. Just in case the seats are all taken. Cars are usually packed."

"Fine," Shaw said. "I'll have the fare by then." He paused. "People like you make me feel good about fighting for my country."

"You deserve it, fellow," the agent said. "Giving an arm and all."

*   *   *

He had to get the fare. Had he been a little quicker he might have latched onto one of the freight cars hauling the show equipment, he thought, but once the train was moving he had stood no chance.

Not with only one arm. To try would have meant almost certain death under the wheels.

It was dark now, and he judged his best chance was to stake out a spot near a saloon somewhere and keep an eye on departing drinkers. Try to mug a staggering drunk, if possible, and hope he had some money.

Even that wouldn't be easy, not like that time in Mina when he'd knocked out that unwary gambler with a rock to get the rail fare to Tonopah for him and his now-dead partners.

He had hit his victim over the head with a heavy rock then, because he'd had no other weapon. He had a gun now, but he wanted to avoid firing it. A shot might well bring a rushing crowd out of a saloon, depending on how much reckless courage they had imbibed.

He would use the gun, but only as a sap to fell his prey. Right over the ear was best, he thought. Swing hard, and swing accurate. With only one arm, he couldn't afford to miss. Then slip away unnoticed. Don't attract attention, lay low till train time in the morning.

He found a good hiding place on a narrow dark street. Directly across from a saloon, he took up vigil.

He watched and waited. He realized it was early in the evening for heavy saloon trade, but he needed to be in position to strike at the right time.

Men walked in and out of the saloon.

He began to worry that his prolonged presence there might be observed by some alert and curious passerby, although he was pretty well hidden between two closely adjacent wood structures.

A couple of hours passed. He grew tired and was about to abandon his post when he saw a large figure burst drunkenly out of the saloon and stagger into the middle of the street. The man stood there swaying, as if undecided about which direction to take.

It was the chance Shaw had been waiting for. He moved from his concealment, and slipping to one side so as to approach from behind the figure, he closed in quickly. His gun was in hand and raised to sideswipe the man's skull.

He swung hard, slamming the weapon's barrel against a temple.

Nothing happened.

Nothing except that the big figure turned and grabbed at him. Shaw jumped backward, but not far enough.

A second later long powerful arms had him in a bearlike embrace that squeezed him breathless.

His arm was imprisoned against his side; only the wrist was free, holding the gun.

In wild panic, he twisted the gun up and squeezed the trigger.

The .45 slug tore into the man's thigh. The suffocating hug loosened, and he went down in a heap.

The door of the saloon was flung open, and patrons crowded there, trying to peer out.

Shaw instinctively glanced toward the saloon and saw them. One or two had already pushed through, staring into the shadows.

Shaw looked at the crumpled figure and saw a dropped wallet beside the man. He shoved his gun into his slung valise, ducked low to snatch up the wallet, then turned and slipped back through the space where he had hidden.

Behind him he heard yells as the saloon crowd reached the wounded figure in the street.

Someone yelled, "It's Big Sanson, and he's shot!"

Shaw cleared the narrow passage between the buildings and broke into a dead run.

He ran blindly through the back streets, still clutching the wallet, wanting to be rid of it but unable to remove the contents one-handed.

Gradually he slowed, aware now that none of the saloon patrons were pursuing him.

He finally paused several blocks away and close enough to a lighted window to examine what the billfold held.

He was gladly surprised to find greenbacks in an amount to pay his train fare and considerably more. He shoved them into a pocket and discarded the wallet into some nearby rubbish.

He went on, this time walking and looking for a place to spend the rest of the night. At first he thought of returning to the rail depot but quickly changed his mind.

Best to stay clear of there for now, he thought. There just might be a limited search for the attacker of the big saloon patron. It would be better to keep out of sight, although those who found the victim were probably concerned more with getting him to a doctor than hunting for whoever shot him. Shaw felt almost certain the man would survive.

The bastard had been almost a giant, Shaw told himself. Shaw was a big man himself and hadn't given much thought to the size of his prey. Not until he'd felt himself in the squeeze of those powerful arms.

The incident was another painful reminder to Shaw that he was no longer the man physically he had been. And it was all Drake's fault.

Right at that moment he came abreast of a poster pasted to the side of a corner building.

He halted to stare at it and cursed to himself. There the son of a bitch was, gunhand extended and shooting an apple off somebody's head!

He had to fight down an urge to draw his own gun and blast away at the poster.

Well, Drake's time would come soon.

With that thought firmly in his mind, he walked on past the poster and found an alley to sleep in.

At first light he awoke, cold and stiff, from a fitful sleep. Shaw made his way to the rail station.

The agent was already on duty and greeted him warmly. "Did you find your friend?" he asked.

"I sure did," Shaw said, trying to match the agent's tone. He took out the currency he had robbed, and peeled off the amount of the fare to Goldfield.

The agent handed him the ticket. "Be a wait," he said. "You're a little early."

"I was afraid you'd forget me," Shaw said. "About holding a seat and all."

The agent said, "I never forget a war hero when I meet one."

"It's good to meet a patriot," Shaw said.

An hour later he was seated on the train, which was, as the agent had predicted, crowded. But he was on his way again.

And this time, by God! that trick shot son of a bitch wasn't going to slip away.

In Reno, three days later, the man the saloon patron had called Big Sanson was recovering fairly well from the wound that had come close to gelding him.

The Reno deputy sheriff dropped by his rented room to check on his condition. Sanson had previously managed to give him a description of the attacker: a big man, not as big as Sanson, with a black beard.

"Scant on details," the deputy had initially remarked.

"That's about all I can tell you," Sanson had said. "It was too dark."

Today this was just a friendly visit by the lawman because he and Sanson were casually acquainted. The deputy had already written off the attack as just another mugging in the tenderloin district. It wasn't something to spend a lot of time and effort on. Muggings were not infrequent in the area.

"Glad to see you're coming along all right," the deputy said.

Sanson's big frame was sprawled out on his bed.

"Yeah, I ain't hurting too bad now. The wound, at least. But I'm plenty griped at letting it happen."

"Well, you said he was a big son of a bitch," the lawman said.

"Not nearly as big as me."

"Even so," the deputy said.

Sanson's anger seemed to flare at the remark, and he blurted out, "But with only one arm!"

"Only one arm?"

Sanson suddenly looked embarrassed. "Dammit! I let that slip out!"

"Why the hell didn't you tell me that before when I asked you to describe him?"

Sanson was silent.

"Well?" the lawman said.

"Dammit!" Sanson said. "How'd you like to be a man my size and have to admit you was overcome by a jasper that has one arm missing?"

The deputy thought about that for a moment, then said, "Yeah, I see what you mean."

Later that day, the railroad station agent got word to the deputy's office that he had something to discuss with him about a recent mugging he'd heard about.

In due time the lawman stopped by the depot.

"Glad to see you," the agent said. "A rumor has got around that the Sanson mugging a few days back was done by a one-armed attacker."

"That's right," the deputy said. "I spread the story myself just as soon as I found out. Hoping in might help to identify who did it."

"I think it can, Sheriff." The agent hesitated, then said, "It could have been the war hero."

"What do you mean—war hero?"

"Fellow that said he'd lost his arm charging up San Juan Hill."

"He buy a ticket to somewhere?"

"Sure did. To Goldfield. He was dead set on seeing that Wild West show, after missing it here."

The lawman phoned Sheriff Ingalls in Goldfield, requesting he watch for a black-bearded suspect with one arm who might show up at the exhibition grounds.

Sheriff Ingalls was a lean, gray, elderly man. He had been the Esmeralda County sheriff for many years, based up in Hawthorne long before Goldfield came into existence.

Now he was based in Goldfield and had business interests in the mining town that partly occupied his time. They included ownership of the Palace Saloon, above which he had his offices, and it was rumored he had cribs in the tenderloin section that he rented to the whores.

This could have been the reason for his lack of zealous response to the request for action by the law officer in Reno. The fact was he was not too interested in trying to apprehend some incompetent mugger who had bungled an attack on a half-drunk victim. An attack that had done no more than wound the victim in the leg.

Reno was a long way from Goldfield, up in a different county, and the sheriff's interests these days were locally focused. But he did send two deputies to scout the showgrounds.

They eventually reached the show site as it was ready to open and the crowds were moving in.

"How the hell," one asked the other, "do we find a suspect from the descriptions we was given?"

"Long black beard and missing right arm," his partner said.

"There's a lot of black-bearded bastards in a crowd this big. You see any with one arm?"

"You can't always tell for sure. There's one-armed fellows sometimes get a false arm attached, just to fill their coat sleeve."

"That don't make our job any easier."

"For sure," his companion said. "Hey, that might be one over there now. You see how he keeps his hand in his pocket? That's another sign sometimes. May be a false hand."

"Let's ask him."

"Ask him, hell!" The one who spoke, who was bigger than average, stepped out and stopped the passerby.

The man looked startled and said, "Hey!"

The deputy grabbed his right sleeve and gave it a hard twist.

The man yelped in pain.

The deputy said, "That arm real?"

The man stared at his badge, then at his face. "Are you crazy?" he said "Let go of it and I'll show you how real it is. Right across your frigging face."

"Listen, buster, this is the law you're talking to."

"Well, by god, if it is, I'd hate to meet the lawless."

The other deputy said to the one still holding the arm, "I don't think this is him."

"It appears so."

The passerby said, "I ought to report you to the management. This kind of treatment is going to drive away business fast."

"Sorry about it." The deputy holding the arm let go of it. "Just trying to do my job."

The man smoothed his crumpled coat sleeve.

"Anybody ever tell you you're in the wrong line of work," he said.

Jack Shaw had been waiting for the right time.

Now it was here.

He had made a couple of efforts to enter the show grounds while it was being readied. The first time he was turned away by roustabouts who warned him there was no admittance on the site to outsiders.

Wanting to arouse no suspicions, he did not argue.

The second time, a day later, he slipped by them but found himself temporarily lost before being accosted by a security guard who promptly escorted him to the gate.

"Come back after we're ready," the guard told him, "and buy a ticket. We don't allow nobody roaming around here where they might get hurt."

Again, Shaw figured he'd gain nothing by protest.

So he decided to follow the guard's advice: He'd wait and get a ticket to the first performance.

On the following day the show would open, and Shaw would be in line early to get admitted.

His original plan had been to catch Drake alone, maybe after a rehearsal, and confront him. Just the two of them. Now he thought of another way to pay Drake back. It would require that he be close to the front row.

And in the right location.

CHAPTER 18

WITH THE SHOW set up at Goldfield, problems arose immediately as Drake and Castle ran through a brush-up routine at the new location.

Castle's flinching returned.

Drake had worked with enough show people to know there were two types. There were those, like himself, with specialty acts that required dexterity on which they prided themselves, much as a tradesman would. There were others who lived on their ability to express emotions—actors.

Neither type of performer was worth his salt if he lost his nerve. That's what had happened to Gilbert Castle, Drake thought.

"Dammit!" Drake said. "Gil, you've become gun shy!"

Gilbert's expressive face showed a sadness. He could not deny it, did not reply at all. He merely nodded.

"Why now?" Drake said. "You've been doing well since that one time back there in Reno."

"John, I don't know. After that other time I shoved all thought of a misfire out of my mind. And kept it out."

Drake was silent, considering this, then said, "And now that thought is returning to you and you can't hold it back?"

"It's worse than that," Castle said.

"How worse?"

"I'm flinching now reflexively. Without any thought of why."

"And you're making me miss."

Castle said then, "I think it's because we'll be performing here in Goldfield, where *it* happened."

Drake was silent. He too had been haunted by the memory of that tragedy more than usual since his return to Goldfield.

Finally, he said, "Day after tomorrow, we go on before a crowd. The featured act. Get hold of yourself, Gil."

"I will," Gilbert said.

But there was something in his voice that left Drake uncertain whether to believe him. They took a short break, then resumed their rehearsal.

"Let's run through some of it again," Drake said.

"Sure," Gilbert said.

"Let's start with the clay pigeons, you holding," Drake said.

Castle went to a table, picked up a pair, and walked over to one of the backstops. With arms extended, he held a clay pigeon at each side, shoulder high.

Drake drew a show pistol from his fancy *buscadero* belt and holster, and fired two fast shots.

The clay bird in Castle's right hand shattered. The one in his left required another shot.

Gilbert said, "I'm sorry, John. I must have moved the second one."

"You did," Drake said.

"Could we get the same effect if I held them in short split sticks?"

Drake frowned and said, "You know better than that."

"Yeah, you're right."

"Let's try the lighted-candle snuff-out, you holding it aloft."

Gilbert picked up a two-foot-long metal channel with a dozen candles fixed upright in it. Drake lighted them, and Castle carried it to the backstop and held it by its ends, a foot above his head.

Drake immediately grabbed a pistol in either hand and began blasting out the flames, working in from either end.

With half the number extinguished, Castle's arms

seemed to weaken slightly, and in a split second lost as Drake compensated, two bullets missed, leaving two candles burning.

Two candles still flaming, and both revolvers empty.

Drake tried to fight down his frustration. "Use your breath to blow them out," he said to Castle, in a hard, flat voice.

Castle did so, keeping his eyes averted.

"Twelve candles too heavy for you to hold?" Drake said.

"It wasn't the weight, John. It was a muscle jerk I couldn't control."

"It only happens when you're holding targets for me," Drake said. "Try another trick, Gil."

"Which one?"

"The one we save for the last. The cigarette in the mouth."

Castle did not move.

Drake studied him, then said, "You know how to light a cigarette, don't you?"

Castle remained silent.

"We've done it successfully for weeks, Gil."

This time Gil spoke. He said, "But not here in Goldfield, John."

Drake hesitated, then said, "Exactly why I want to be sure of it."

Abruptly, as if driven, Castle took a cigarette from a pack on the table, moved to the backstop, struck a match, and lighted it.

He struck his pose, profile to Drake, the cigarette in his lips.

Drake studied him for a moment, and was almost certain he could see a tenseness in the jaw line that he'd not seen before.

He aimed his gun and fired.

And missed as Castle jerked back his head.

*   *   *

It was Bonner who brought word to Winston of the trouble Drake was having with Castle.

He was surprised when Winston did not seem upset. Instead, he was uncharacteristically calm when he asked, "Got a return of what he briefly had in Reno, eh?"

Bonner nodded. "It appears so. And Drake is near out of his mind, what with an actual performance coming up day after tomorrow."

"Tell me, is Drake's girl aware of this?"

"Of course. She's always there watching. And she's as concerned as Drake himself is."

"It's time then to broach the subject again," the boss said. "I want to use the girl as Drake's assistant."

"As I said before, Drake is not likely to agree to it."

"Major, he's got a contract to live up to. If Castle can't be the target, Henie will have to do it!"

"But the agreement between Drake and me," Bonner said, "was that Henie would not be part of the act."

"There's nothing in the written contract to spell that out. I made a point of checking to see."

Bonner was silent. Then he said, "Hal, I don't like this."

Winston, who was standing close to him, reached out a hand and laid it on his shoulder, and said, "Major, at times we all do things that we do not like—for the good of the business we're in. I daresay it's happened to you often enough in your previous career as a military officer."

"That's not the same thing," Bonner said. "Whatever I did, I was following orders."

Winston gave him a long, hard stare before he said, "Feel the same way about this, if you like."

"I'll tell him," Bonner said, "but Drake may not agree, contract or not."

"Then maybe I'd better handle Drake myself," Winston said. "Aside from his singular expertise, he is basically a showman. One to whom I have restored a career. You can tell by his recent performances that he is beginning to relish the return of the applause he formerly had."

"That may not be enough," Bonner said.

"We'll soon see," Winston said.

Winston himself showed up in Drake's quarters. Henie was present when he did.

Winston, usually genial in his greetings, now wore a worried frown. After a brief nod to each of them, he wasted no time in making known the reason for his visit.

He said, "Bonner tells me that Castle has had a return of his jitters."

Drake seemed hesitant to reply, and it was Henie who answered.

"That's true, Mr. Winston."

Drake spoke then. "I've been hoping he would get over them, as he did before."

"And?"

"He hasn't," Henie said.

Winston let them have a short silence to reflect on their own words. Then he said, "You realize that a change must be made."

"A change to whom?" Drake said. "I'm thinking possibly of Henie's brother, Tagee. You know he is working with the show as a roustabout. He might be trained as Castle was."

"There is no time for that," Winston said flatly. "We've publicized your act heavily here in Goldfield. People here have a special interest in seeing your comeback performance. As a showman yourself, you must understand that."

Drake was silent, considering his words, knowing what he meant.

Winston studied him briefly, then as Drake was about to speak, Winston turned to Henie and said quickly, "You have watched the act, day after day. You are familiar with the routine. As an understudy, so to speak in theatrical terms. And it is you who can be the one to save John's performance here from being a failure. Are you willing?"

Without hesitation, Henie said, "Yes, gladly."

He turned immediately back to Drake.

"Here is your solution, John. Your chance to prove you are completely over the past and at the peak of your shooting skill. The crowds will love you!"

He stopped speaking then, seeing he had touched on Drake's performance ego. He had dealt with performing people for years, and he knew what it was that made them tick.

He let a long silence hang, his eyes on Drake.

"Are you sure you want to do this?" Drake said, turning to Henie.

"Yes, John," she said.

Winston looked at her and at that moment was startled by her enthusiasm. She wasn't saying this only for Drake's sake. It was obvious to him: *The girl herself is stagestruck!*

The thought made him smile.

CHAPTER 19

THERE HE WAS, before a record crowd of expectant watchers, and his own nerve began to fail him.

This even as he began the less difficult parts of his act. His and Henie's act now.

He had made two trial runs with her the previous day and was surprised that she did her part flawlessly. Surprised too that so did he.

But that was in private, without the hundreds of people filling the stands, watching him with expectant eyes. Now he had to fight his own nerves to keep from being overwhelmed.

He was losing the fight: Everywhere he looked and everything he did brought back the memory of that awful moment on the stage at the Hippodrome, here in Goldfield.

Tagee was out there, too. Drake had spotted him early, seated a few rows back in the stands, several yards to the left of the marked-out ring where Drake and Henie and their bullet-stopping backboards and paraphernalia were placed.

Drake wondered if Tagee had asked time off from his roustabout duties in order to watch his sister's performance. Tagee had made no secret of his constant concern for his sister's well-being.

Drake's glance paused briefly on the figure of a large man with a coat draped loosely over his broad shoulders. He was sitting closer to the ring than Tagee, in the second row.

It was warm in the tent, and the coat seemed out of place.

There was something else there that momentarily held Drake's attention before his eyes continued scanning the crowd. Something vaguely familiar.

Tagee had a handgun hidden in a shoulder holster under his loose-fitting work shirt. He had objected strongly to Henie's becoming Drake's target assistant.

His protests had been ignored.

He felt angry and defeated, but he knew of nothing else he could do.

Not at that time.

But he had brooded about it and was finally driven to a mad decision.

If all went well, he would do nothing. But if harm came to Henie . . .

An usher had directed Shaw to the particular ring in which the famed trick shot, Drake, would perform.

"Great act," the usher had replied to Shaw's inquiry. "Saw it twice myself recently in Reno. It may be even better now. He's got a good-looking girl holding targets for him now."

"The hell!" Shaw said, surprised.

"You'll have a lot of other entertainment first," the usher said. "You'll note on that program you got that he's the final and featured act."

"I'll look forward to it," Shaw said, managing to grab a seat in the second row. He sat there, absently rubbing his jowls from which he had scissor-shortened his beard the previous evening, leaving only a stubble.

He had judged the stubble to be an approximation of what he'd had when he traded bullets with Drake.

He knew what he'd done had some risk, but he had it set in his mind that the son of a bitch should recognize who was killing him. It had become an obsession he did not try to shake. Meanwhile he sat with a coat draped over his shoulders to hide the fact of his missing arm until he chose to show it. He was hoping that not until then would Drake know him.

At last there was Drake in the designated spot for his performance. And despite the words of the usher revealing a woman assistant now taking part, Shaw was startled to see it was the Paiute girl.

He had read in a news account that she had been with Drake during his recovery, but had never expected she would be the woman in his act.

He was startled and upset. When the bullets started to fly she might be hit.

It bothered Shaw that he would even care about what happened to her. His concern for her might affect his aim. He would have to delay his own move to a time when she would be out of danger.

Despite all that had happened, the thought of what might have been had he reached Arizona with her struck him hard.

He cursed to himself. This was no time to think of that.

Drake had made only a few preliminary shots, then came to a change in the routine, influenced by Henie's prior advice. She had said, "John, you are troubled most by the cigarette-shooting trick. Because of what once happened. And that is the shot your audience wants most strongly to see. I say make the shot early on and get it over, then you can relax for the rest of the act."

"I'm thinking of deleting it," he had said. "The hell with the audience."

"Forget the audience then," she said. "But do the shot for your own sake."

He had finally agreed and scheduled it after a few easier warm-up tricks.

Now they had come to that point in the repertoire.

He walked toward a small table where there were several preloaded light-caliber revolvers. Henie took her position and struck her pose with the lighted cigarette in her lips.

Facing her at twenty feet, Drake picked up his weapon from the table, flicking a glance to the nearest spectators.

He saw the big man in the second row, the same man he had previously noticed. He saw the man rise and shed the coat that had draped his shoulders. Drake looked squarely at the big man, who now raised a gun, pointed at Drake. The man lifted a stump where the lower arm had been amputated.

Suddenly Drake recalled the escaped convict riding off, his shattered arm dangling at his side.

He knew Shaw read the recognition on his face as he squeezed the trigger of a big .45 aimed at him. Simultaneously, Drake fired the .32 caliber show pistol at Shaw, sighting instinctively, knowing that to be effective he must put a bullet in a mortally effective spot.

The roar of Shaw's heavier gun drowned out that of the lighter one, his bullet driving into the ground between the shooters.

Shaw stood for a moment before he fell, standing just long enough that Drake saw he had put a bullet into one of Shaw's eyes. Shaw went down, no doubt dead before he hit the ground.

A few women were screaming. Some people were running out or scrambling to get under the bleachers.

The spectators near Shaw were on their feet, staring down at the corpse.

Drake turned away and looked for Henie.

There she stood, once again in ready pose. She caught his stare and gave him a slight nod, but no other movement.

He knew what she meant, but he stood there hesitating, his pistol at his side.

Members of the crowd grew gradually quiet, as their attention shifted back to the ring. Shocked and confused, even those standing by Shaw's body looked silently at Drake and Henie. No one moved.

It came to Drake that an eye at twenty yards was a shot much harder to hit than a cigarette at twenty feet.

He raised his pistol and fired. The cigarette she was holding in her lips was extinguished by the bullet.

She turned, met his eyes, and smiled. Drake knew then that with one shot he had regained what he thought he had lost forever when Molly died—a future and someone to share it with.